AF317017

Neurosis

**NASH
NELSON**

Thank you to everyone who purchased this book! Your support means everything to me. :)

R.I.P. Paris. The rainbow bridge has its hands full with you, little buddy.

Also, feel free to visit my Patreon page! URL is patreon.com/nashnelson :)

Also, another huge THANK YOU to Laurel 'Artimis' Adkins for designing the cover for this book. Check out her work here: https://www.deviantart.com/xxartimisxx

CONTENTS

NEUROSIS

"The same feeling of not belonging, of futility, wherever I go: I pretend interest in what matters nothing to me, I bestir myself mechanically or out of charity, without ever being caught up, without ever being somewhere. What attracts me is elsewhere, and I don't know where that elsewhere is."

-Emil Cioran

| one |

Silver Lining?

"Just sign here and you're all set to go," said Dr. Holland as she handed me one final sheet to release me from my captivity. I took the pen from off the gray countertop and signed my John Hancock. "Thank you," she commented happily, eager to see me leave her pale white psych ward, no doubt. I wasn't her worst patient, by far. But I'm sure she wasn't too pleased to deal with a patient with my particular set of problems.

"Is anyone coming to pick me up?" I asked as I set the pen back onto the counter.

"You'll need to call somebody," she said, blinking her green eyes. "I think you have your friend Maron listed as an emergency contact."

I smiled. Maron was good people. She was the one person who seemed to care that I was having hard troubles within my corrupted brain. Maron certainly wasn't my keeper, but she occasionally checked in with me to make sure I was okay. It was her who drove me to that hospital, actually.

"Thank you, Doctor," I said with a grin. "May I have the phone so I can call her?"

"Of course," she responded, sharing a smile of her own with me as she handed me the white telephone from off the nurse's station. I took the phone and dialed Maron's number.

The other end rang twice before my friend answered. *"Hello?"*

"Hey Maron," I greeted with a sigh. "It's Melbourne. I-I'm being discharged."

She squealed happily. *"That's wonderful! I'll pick you up now. I'll be there in ten, fifteen minutes tops."*

I nodded slowly. "Okay. I'll be outside waiting." We said our good-byes and I pressed the red button, ending the call. "Thank you, Doctor. May I go now?" The elderly woman nodded, handing over the brown bag that contained my phone, medications, clothes, and toiletries. Once she pressed the big white button on the countertop, the electric door swung open.

"Enjoy your new beginning, sir."

I cringed at the incorrect referral, but said nothing to correct her. After all, she was old and likely stuck in her ways. "Thank you," I muttered as I stepped through the open doorway. Within a matter of seconds, I was outside the hospital.

I was free, but for how long?

I was diagnosed with schizoaffective disorder; the bipolar subtype, to be exact. I came to the Fairfield Behavioral Hospital after planning for months on how I could jump off a building and meet my fatal end. I had a particular building selected, and it was going to be my safe haven from the wretched world. I even had a timeframe planned out and everything.

However, I then realized that the height of the building wouldn't have been enough to kill me, but rather brutally injure me. I'd be forced to pay a hefty hospital bill, deal with the scorn of my family and friends, and possibly be expelled from school. So I decided to give up on the plan and check myself into the hospital.

And honestly?

I still felt rather depressed, even after four days of intensive therapy and medication administration.

However, I at least knew what name to refer to my problems as. I had the tools to sort out my mental health and prevent another low episode from occurring. Granted, I also had to watch out for highs, too. I was expected to be on a plain, no special moods lifting me up or holding me down.

It sounded like a dreadfully boring existence.

But if that's what was demanded for my mental health, so be it.

Clutching my bag, I looked up at the sky and breathed in the fresh air away from the musty atmosphere of the hospital. The sky was as blue as a newborn's eyes, the clouds forming what looked like a unicorn frolicking over a field of flowers. The breeze outside engulfed me like a shawl, knitted to perfection by a doting grandmother. A nearby business appeared to be hosting a company barbeque; I could tell by the smell of charcoal and sizzling meat that wafted into my nostrils.

Before I knew it, a large bug landed itself on the tip of my nose. "Oh? Hello there, friend." From a quick glance, I figured out it was either a butterfly or a moth. The creature slid its little feet across my skin, tickling me. Once my new friend was done visiting, it flew away, turning its back to me. A yellow skull greeted me on the bug's back. "Unusual," I commented aloud. "Oh well."

The goodbye was too fast, but I still smiled.

It was still a beautiful Monday afternoon.

I was bruised in the heart, but such a lovely day lifted my spirits significantly.

The first lesson I was taught in the ward was to look at the beauty in everything. Not everything was total shit like my depression suggested. If anything, the world was more majestic than my feeble, self-centered mind allowed me to believe. I would begin to believe it once I found evidence proving the statement to be factual.

Of course, Maron's presence certainly assisted in doing so. Her red Jeep turned into the parking lot, stopping in front of me. The blonde rolled down her window and smiled at me. "Hey cutie. You need a ride?"

I grinned, grabbing a hold of the door handle. "Yes, sexy taxi driver. Take me away from this place."

"Get in then, dumbass," she said with a playful giggle. "The others will want to know you're doing okay."

Wasting no time, I opened the passenger-side door and climbed into the vehicle. After buckling up and closing my door, Maron sped away from Fairfield Behavioral Hospital. Some nineties grunge played on her radio, despite it being the year 2024. She liked old stuff like that, and I'd be lying if I said I didn't get any mild enjoyment from it as well. It helped when there was music I liked.

"You hungry?" Maron asked as her eyes watched the road in front of her. "I can't imagine they fed you well in that hospital."

I rolled my eyes. "Oh yeah," I snarked, looking over at my friendly driver. "Nothing quite hits the spot like undercooked sloppy joe."

"My God," Maron drawled. "Yeah, I'm getting you something to eat. But first, we should probably check in with the others. How does lunch at the cafe sound?"

I nodded slowly. "That sounds fine to me."

An awkward moment of silence fell before us, music filling the void. I knew what she was thinking, and I wasn't sure I was prepared to answer her questions. When one hears that somebody has a psychotic disorder, they tend to pull away. At least, that's what I'd always heard. It was probably why people far worse off than I am were often homeless.

"So," she said, finally gathering the courage to speak up. "How are you holding up, Mel? You were in a pretty bad way the other day. How do you feel now?"

I sighed, looking through my side window at the passing buildings. "Better, I suppose. Not really suicidal anymore."

Maron nodded, smiling weakly. "That's great. You have so much to live for. You're in school for fucking counseling! You have a great future ahead of you."

I smirked. "Yeah, I suppose so."

"There's no "suppose" to it, Melbourne," Maron argued. "You're compassionate. You don't need to let the drudgery of the world bring you down."

Biting my bottom lip, I refrained from arguing with my friend. She meant well, she really did. It wasn't her fault that she didn't know the fullest extent of what was going through my mind. Perhaps I'd tell her one day.

One day.

"You're right," I said rather insincerely. "I will work on myself and not let the world bring me down."

"There you go," Maron responded happily. "You got this, buddy. Don't ever forget that." Before I knew it, we were pulling into the parking lot of our college campus. It was roughly about two o'clock in the afternoon, so most of the parking spots were taken up by commuters. "Ugh, I hate the parking here," Maron groaned.

"Tell me about it," I sighed.

As we pulled up to the main building, I smiled. My friends, Johnny and Kimberly, were standing by the entrance, chatting each other up as they always did. They were such a cute couple. I longed for a relationship like theirs one day.

"Here," Maron commented, shifting the car into park. "I'll let you out. I'm going to look for parking. I'll see you soon."

I unbuckled my seatbelt and climbed out of the car. I ran over to Johnny and Kimberly, who must've heard my rough breathing. Before they could properly react, I pulled Johnny into a tight hug. "I missed you guys!"

The muscular red-headed man grunted within my embrace, pulling away. "Melbourne? What's gotten into you?"

My smile fought the temptation to drop, and I shrugged. "I-I've been gone for a few days. I figured you guys would've wondered where I was."

The brunette woman beside Johnny shrugged. "It's none of our business what you do in your spare time, Melbourne. Besides, we've been busy with school work."

At her words, I frowned. "Oh. I see."

"Yeah," Kimberly continued. "My mom has been on my ass about my grades. Johnny's dad, too. They don't want us to see each other anymore."

I felt my heart sink in my chest. I'd been gone for four days after being an inch away from killing myself, and my friends didn't seem to care about any of that. True, they had their own issues to contend with. But still, wouldn't they have at least tried to care about my well-being?

Isn't that what friends were supposed to do?

And so, Johnny and Kimberly started filling me in on their troubles. I listened intently, but my mood went sour again. The little hope I had felt earlier seemed to dissipate. My own trials and tribulations didn't seem to matter; not when everyone else had their own troubles they were going through.

There wasn't much of a silver lining for me, it seemed.

| two |

Singing in the Walls

Soft mumblings rumbled throughout my apartment, a woman's voice humming a tune that only I could hear. My flatmates were out, so it was only me and the song of my madness. I sat on the couch of the living room, trying desperately to make out what this mysterious woman was singing. I couldn't make out the rhythm, as it seemed to be all over the place.

Dark anger, then light joy.

Deep voice followed by higher pitches.

Lyrics that couldn't figure out their end goal.

Hence the story of my life.

After having lunch with Maron, I retreated back to my home base so I could process what had happened to me over the last few days. The school might've not been the best, but that apartment was my sanctuary. It was the one place I could rest and enjoy loneliness. Not that being alone was necessarily the best thing for me right at that moment, but still.

After the way Johnny and Kimberly had brushed me off, I didn't feel like human interaction was for me. Anger coursed through my body. I just got out of the hospital, and yet my issues were a non-issue to others. Perhaps it was selfish of me to impose my sorrow onto others, but a little support and compassion would've gone a long way.

Perhaps they didn't truly care about me as I did them?

Perhaps they wanted to see me die?

Maybe they were upset that I didn't follow through with my plan?

I suppose I was being paranoid, but that wasn't anything new to me. Paranoia was my eternal lover. We made love every night, though it was never consensual. I never wanted its touch, but I got it anyway. Everyone was out to get me, and I was doomed to die a horrific death. But I was expected to keep others from following suit or else I'd be a terrible human being. How fucked up was that?

"You are alone," said the woman living in the walls. *"You'll always be alone."*

That wasn't true, I told myself.

It couldn't be.

I had Maron and my family.

She was just trying to psych me out, was all.

I'd been told multiple times in my life by different psychiatric specialists that I had a psychotic disorder. When I was a kid, a counselor told me I was schizophrenic because I still had an imaginary friend in the fifth grade. I paid no mind to her, of course. I was a lonely child. How could that be equated to madness?

Then there was another time in high school that a counselor suggested I had schizophrenia because I was chronically paranoid. Again, I ignored this assessment. I was bullied all the time. I had every right to be paranoid.

It seemed that I now had an official diagnosis.

I guess the joke was on me.

Things that I never even thought were symptoms were signs of my disorder all along. There was my anhedonia, or lack of pleasure. There was also my avolition, or lack of motivation. Not to be forgotten, I had flat emotions; oh Christ, the flat emotions!

There were also the positive symptoms, such as hallucinations, paranoia, and delusional thought content. I remember always being in denial about hallucinating. I never hallucinated. Me? Never!

Only I did.

I just never realized it.

The truth was undeniable; I was a psycho. I was clinically crazy. I'd forever be lumped into the same group as all the school shooters who were also diagnosed with some kind of psychiatric affliction. If I ever acted out of turn, everyone would just roll their eyes and call me "that lunatic." I'd never be taken seriously ever again.

I sighed. "What am I going to do?"

Then, a lightbulb went off in my head. Perhaps I didn't need to be alone. Maybe if I just explained my problems to others, they'd understand and I'd be heard and understood. I'd tell my friends and family! Yes! That's precisely what I was going to do!

I grabbed my cell phone from off the coffee table and searched for my mother's phone number in my contacts. Upon finding her, I clicked the green button and held the phone up to my ear. The phone rang once before her voice graced my ears. *"Hello?"*

"Hey Mom," I breathed. "How are you?"

"Melbourne!" she exclaimed. *"It's so wonderful to hear from you! We were just talking about you."*

My eyes widened. "Oh?"

"Yes," she said. *"We were talking about how you're in school to be a therapist and how it's the coolest thing ever!"*

I sighed.

Good, it wasn't anything bad.

"I see," I said calmly. "Look Mom, I need to talk to you guys about something. Can I come over tonight?"

She giggled. *"You don't need to ask, Melbourne. You're always welcome here. But, don't you have homework you need to do?"*

I shook my head, despite her not being able to see me at that present moment. "Nah. I, uh, don't have any tonight."

"Oh, good!" she commented. *"Then yes, you can come over. We'll be eagerly awaiting your arrival."*

I smiled. "Thanks, Mom. I'll head over right now. Love you," I hung up the call and leaned back into the couch. "Here goes nothing, I guess." As I stood up from the couch to go grab my car keys, the lady in the walls had one last thing to tell me.

"You're wasting your time."

I shook my head again. "You're wrong. My family loves me. They'll understand where I'm coming from. Just wait and see."

At that moment, I slapped my forehead.

I was talking to the walls.

Fucking *walls*!

Ignoring whatever else the woman had to say, I grabbed my keys from off the counter and stepped outside of the apartment. As I walked to my car, I prepared myself for the very hard conversation I was to have with my family. How would I break the news? How would I explain myself to them? Would they understand where I was coming from?

Only time would tell.

| three |

Time with the Family

My family lived about an hour away from campus. The drive itself wasn't too terrible, just lots of trees and pick-up trucks. The city was behind me, shrouded by countryside woes. People said that southern hospitality was like no other, and they were right; just not in the way they think.

They couldn't understand gender identities aside from man and woman.

They couldn't understand mental health to save their lives, either.

I tried my best to ignore the shadows dancing in my peripheral vision as I drove down the backroad of bumfuck nowhere. Their waltz was enticing, of course. The way they swayed in the sunset's glare made my heart break asunder.

It wasn't real.

None of it was real.

Beauty in madness was merely a deleterious farce.

I was but a milquetoast larva in a swarm of angry wasps. Get my family talking about anything beyond their comprehension and they let the world have it. But hey, at least they were polite in every other sense of the word. Mom cooked a mean pot roast with mashed potatoes.

As I turned on one more road, my parents' house was within sight. A line of rickety shacks didn't ache my desensitized eyes. Even the rusty barn doors greeted me like an old friend. My folks never were one to keep up with the mechanical nature of today. They still had a landline in their home; a technology that had gone obsolete back in the late 90s, early 2000s.

Going to talk to my family about my mental health was likely going to be a waste of time, but I needed to talk to someone. I couldn't just keep the bombshell to myself. I mean, it wasn't everyday one was diagnosed with a debilitating mental illness. Besides, Maron was next on my list of people to confess to; perhaps even Kimberly and Johnny, as well.

I pulled into my parents' driveway, parking up beside the rusty barn right of the house. Rosco, our ten-year-old schnauzer, barked to his little heart's content as he recognized my car. Once I killed the engine, I opened my door and was immediately pawed at. "Hey, buddy," I murmured to the hairy lug as he jumped up to lick my face. "I missed you, too."

With a deep sigh of anticipation, I unbuckled my seatbelt and gently pushed past Rosco. "Lemme out, doggo." I stood up from the vehicle and closed the door behind me. I looked up at my childhood home, blinking slowly.

Dressed in light dirt around the skirt of the white house, the place looked fairly well for a two-decade-old home. The house was a double-wide trailer; fancy enough to not acquire the scorn of rich folk, but not classy enough to earn me many scholarships. I had to fund my way to school the old-fashioned way; by biting the bullet and taking out loans.

I made my way up the wooden porch, breathing through my nose. "Here we go," I murmured as I took my house key and inserted it into the lock. With one swift turn, the door came open and I let myself inside.

The smell of Mexican chicken curled up inside my nose as I stepped onto the gray carpet. It was a recipe my mom enjoyed cooking every now and then. It was spicy nacho chips, queso, sour cream, and white chicken mixed together, cooked at four-hundred degrees. The melted cheese over the nachos and chicken made eating heavenly. As I stated before, Mom was a great cook.

"Is that Melbourne?" She slid her feet up the linoleum floor so she could see me from the kitchen.

I offered her a small smile. "Hey, Mom."

From behind me, Dad playfully punched my arm. "Hey, Sport! How's my main man doing today?"

I bit my bottom lip, trying to fight off the urge to correct his mis-gendering of me. I would've, but I'd had that conversation with him and Mom multiple times. They didn't get it, and I gave up trying to explain anything. I guess I couldn't blame them; nonbinary was a term I was confused by back in the day, too.

"Oh, you know..."

Before I could finish my statement, my little sister came up behind me and wrapped her arms around my torso. "Mel!"

"Hey Sadie," I said with a smile, caressing her hands with mine. She was only fifteen, but seemed to exude more empathy than most people I knew. If I couldn't tell my parents, then perhaps I could tell her and she'd understand. "How're you doing, kiddo?"

She tightened her grip on me. "Pretty good. I got asked to the Spring Dance."

My eyes widened. "*Oooh!* Did you say yes?"

"Nope," she answered cheerfully. "I wanted his brother to ask me out."

Letting out a fake chuckle, I shook my head. "Look at you, playing the field," I let go of her and she released me from her clutches. I turned to look at her, noticing her brunette hair in a messy bun and her brown eyes shimmering under the living room light. "Is he at least cute?"

Sadie giggled. "Yeah. But his brother has a nicer ass."

"*Sadie,*" Mom scolded. "Manners."

As my sister cackled, my old man looked back at me. "So, you said you had something to talk about with us, Melbourne?"

I held my breath for a moment, exhaling once Mom announced that dinner was ready. We all entered the clean kitchen and took our seats at the rectangular table. Mom sat next to me, across from Dad, and Sadie sat across from me. The Mexican chicken was being served with mashed potatoes and buttered rolls; a match made in heaven, surely.

"Let's say grace," Mom instructed as we all closed our eyes. Dad uttered a quick prayer, thanking God for allowing me to come back home for the meal. As we said our amens, I opened my eyes and served myself some chicken.

"So, what was this big thing you had to tell us, Melbourne?" Dad asked again as he shoveled some mashed potatoes onto his plate. "You're leaving me in suspense here."

I took a small bite of my dinner. I was going to drop the bombshell right there; I promise I was. I was going to come clean about my woes. I was going to tell them what I'd learned about myself. I was going to be completely transparent with my loved ones.

But then, Mom had to open her big mouth. "Hopefully you aren't gay, Son," she said with a giggle. "I hear plenty of those folk are the ones instigating all these shootings lately."

I squinted at her. "I…doubt that," I argued. "Besides, this has nothing to do with that."

"Why would you doubt it?" Dad asked. "The news has made it clear that these people are all mentally ill. Y'all already know what they should do with people like that."

"Stuff them with pills," Mom said. "Not guns."

I glared at both of them. Sadie remained quiet, obviously uncomfortable with the conversation at hand. But I knew I needed to say something. So I at least tried. "You know, things aren't as black and white as you guys like to think. Not all mentally ill people are going to shoot up a shopping mall."

My words fell on deaf ears. They continued to guffaw over the loony gay kids who wanted to shoot up the non-offending straight crowd. The conversation went on for a few minutes, which was long enough for me to abandon ship. My mom eventually looked at me and grinned. "What did you want to say to us, dear?"

I sighed heavily.

"That...I love you guys."

| four |

Back to the Grind

A failed purpose under my belt, I decided to return to school the next day. My adventure to Fairfield Behavioral Hospital had taken up a couple of days worth of homework and studying. I dared not ask my classmates what all I missed; it would all likely be on a test that I'd surely fail. I didn't need that kind of disappointment; not right at that moment.

So instead, I waltzed into class like I was never gone. Like a glove, I fitted in seamlessly; nobody said a word about my absence. Not even my professor batted an eye. Granted, it was possible that he already knew about my hospitalization.

Perhaps that bitch of a guidance counselor told him that I hadn't been taking care of myself. Or whoever the hell reported me to the dean of the school for "making a mockery" of the school's integrity by dressing like a smelly hobo. Had I grown lax on my personal hygiene? Sure. But what was the point in taking care of myself?

I was going to be judged regardless.

Clean or not.

The superficiality of others made me sick.

Perhaps I wasn't meant for this world at all.

Wait.

It wasn't right to think that way.

That's how I ended up in the hospital in the first place.

I took my seat at a table within the classroom. It wasn't a stereotypical college classroom; no wraparounds. I went to a smaller school, so the rooms were more homey and intimate. Friends sat together and cut up during class via text messages and funny faces.

I had no friends during that particular class; all of mine were either in Advanced Mathematics or World History. Psychology 101 was where it was at for me. It was ironic, I know. The mentally ill freak wanted to be a counselor. How would I be able to help others if I couldn't even help myself? I suppose that was the elephant in the room.

Regardless, I knew I needed to persevere through the class if I were to make something out of myself one day. So I sat up straight and sank my teeth into my notes; my outdated notes. I copied down as much information as I could from the last two sections that I seemed to have missed. One was Jung, and the other was Carl Rogers.

Reading a little of each section, I nodded. "Easy enough," I murmured to myself. "I think I got this."

Once the clock hit right at nine o'clock, Dr. Barris stood up and cleared his throat. "Okay, everyone," said the forty-something professor with dark brown hair and a chiseled jawline. "Let's put the phones away and dig into some review."

A sigh of relief washed over me. It seemed like I would get past the lesson unscathed. A part of me wondered if he had done this intentionally for my benefit. I would've greatly appreciated it if he had. It felt like he subtly sent me well wishes without saying a word.

Another part of me said I was reading too much into it. I was connecting dots in which no link was present. Regardless of the why, I was thankful. I vowed to make myself useful in the class by learning all I could.

"Alright," Dr. Barris started out. "Turn to page one-seventy-five." My peers diligently followed his directions. I did not, as I had already been sitting on the chapter about Humanistic Psychology. I leaned back in my seat, staring at the old portrait of Carl Rogers.

"As we discussed yesterday," the teacher explained. "Humanistic Psychology's roots lie in Abraham Maslow's work. The act of self-actualization is a core component in the growth one faces in this counseling approach, or rather the journey to self-actualization. We cannot get through life by doing what we're dutifully told to do. We have to realize our own potential and forge our own path."

Dr. Barris sighed. "You know. Back in my day working as a tech at Fairfield Behavioral Hospital, I found that a more useful approach to treatment was cognitive rational emotive therapy. Can anyone tell me why that might've been the case?"

A handsome stranger raised his hand on the left-hand side of the classroom. I could never remember his name, sad to say.

"Yes?" Dr. Barris asked, calling on the student.

The attractive man cleared his throat. "Because cognitive rational therapy challenges worldviews while the humanistic approach simply facilitates change. The client has to find their own way; regardless if they have the wherewithal to question their own beliefs. Healthcare professionals would prefer to get direct progress, not brain teasers that will further frustrate the client."

The teacher offered a small grin. "Great insight, Tom."

Tom.

That's right.

His name was Tom Baxter.

And there I was, secretly referring to him as Gabriel. Why? Because he was beautiful like an angel of Heaven. Smoldering brown eyes, tan skin, and a buzzcut. His black-rimmed glasses accentuated the freckles underneath his eyes.

He was my dream man and I was sure he felt the same way. I'd seen the way he looked at me. I noticed the gentle tone of voice he'd use to speak with me. I'm sure he didn't really know my name, but I looked to fix that. For a classroom as compact as ours, there was no excuse for us to not be acquainted.

I'd introduce myself once I conquered the tickle in my throat that showed up anytime I was around an attractive person. It didn't matter if they were man, woman, or just like me; beauty was all around me and I just couldn't hold a candle to it all. I wondered if Tom had anything in common with me.

Did he see flickers in raindrops?

How about those who lurked in the shadows?

Did he hear melodic hymns within the walls of his dorm room, too?

If the answer was yes to any of the above, would he be willing to talk about it with me? I wouldn't judge. I wouldn't laugh. I wouldn't scream. I'd take his hand and dance with him as the flickering raindrops rolled off our skins, cooling us as we sang along with the sweet music gracing our ears alone.

But for the time being, I needed the courage to openly acknowledge the admiration he felt for me. And if I ever wanted to get to that point, I needed to use my voice more often than not. So I made the bold move of raising my hand next.

Dr. Barris pointed at me. "Yes, Melbourne?"

I cleared my throat and glanced at Tom from the corner of my eye. With a quick nod, I turned my focus to the teacher. "T-To piggyback off of Tom's point, the humanistic approach also ties into Carl Jung's belief that the human being, as a whole, should be respected; flaws and all," I took a deep breath before continuing. "Wherein a person's flaws lies the ability to rationalize their beliefs, whether for the better or worse. It's kind of a weird dichotomy, if you ask me. We can't ever win."

Satisfied with what I thought was a cogent point, I smiled. Confidence radiated off of me like UV rays from the sun. Everyone looked at me, mesmerized by my words. I'd done it, I thought to myself. I had impressed others. Now people would want to hear more of my thoughts.

Within a few short seconds, however, their faces grew quizzical. It became apparent that they found fault with my answer. My palms began to shake, my heart racing. This was surely rock-bottom; becoming the class fool.

"What," Dr. Barris asked quietly. "What are you even talking about?"

I bit my lip, trying to control my breathing. "S-Sorry," I said breathlessly. "M-Must be w-word salad or s-something."

The teacher blinked, offering no more than a vacant expression on his face. "*Huh?*"

I slapped a hand over my mouth, suddenly feeling sick to my stomach. I quickly jumped out of my seat and bolted out of the classroom. For all of the optimistic talk I was subjected to at Fairfield, nothing seemed to change.

Life was still awful, and I was forever imperfect.

At the rate I was going, it was only a matter of time until I ended up back in that damn hospital.

| **five** |

The Comforting Touch of a Friend

Come lunch time, I was an emotional wreck. The humiliation I'd faced in class was immeasurable. Granted, I'm sure it could've been much worse. At least I didn't cry or have a bowel movement. And maybe I should've taken things in stride.

But man, did it hurt.

My pride ached as if being repeatedly stung by bees. Even the cool air of the outdoors couldn't sate the burning mortification I felt in the pit of my stomach. If I had touched my turkey club sandwich, I might've gotten sick. All my gut could handle at that moment was the stinging nothingness of shame.

Trying desperately to compare Carl Rogers and Carl Jung; what was I thinking?

That was some pseudointellectual nonsense there.

Stupid, stupid, stupid!

As I sat alone at the bench, I stared down at my lunch, partially intending to eat it, but also wanting to toss it into the trash. I'm sure the hard-working cafeteria workers would've been offended by me putting the fruits of their labor to waste, and I was quietly apologetic for even thinking of doing such a thing.

Nevertheless, the last thing I wanted to do was let my nerves get the better of me and cause me to throw up what little food I could stomach. Of course, I was thoroughly convinced the workers were watching me like a hawk. They were waiting for me to take that first bite. Had I thrown their hard work into the garbage bin beside me, I might've been killed.

I didn't want to risk it.

So I sighed and took a small bite out of my lunch.

Exquisite choice of black pepper and cayenne seasoning.

But I wasn't sure I could finish it all.

With a quick inhale through my nostrils, I took another bite. The second bite wasn't as savory and I knew I needed to slow down. Luckily, I had just the right distraction to keep my eyes preoccupied. In my peripheral vision was a large moth fluttering by my head.

Had it been my friend from the other day?

Was it even real?

"Hey there," I greeted with a sheepish voice. "Hope you're having a better day than I am."

The moth squeaked as it floated right in my line of vision. I know it sounds silly, but it felt like this little guy was trying to comfort me from my woes. Or was it a little girl? Or perhaps both, like me?

"If we're going to keep meeting up like this," I stated, taking another small bite out of my sandwich. "Then we need to be on a first name basis. I'm Melbourne."

The moth squeaked again, flying in a little circle.

"What's *your* name, friend?"

The bug looked at me quizzically.

"Do you have a name?"

Another squeak erupted from the moth. I tilted my head in confusion. "Is something wrong, friend? You're making a lot of noise. Normally when creatures do that, they are distressed about something."

With yet another squeak, the insect turned around, revealing its yellow skull imprinted on the back of its thorax. I gave an understanding nod. "I see. You think everyone is afraid of you, don't you? They see the skull and think you're some kind of monster, right?"

With a sigh, I took another bite of my sandwich. "I can relate. Trust me."

The moth turned back to face me, fluttering close to my nose. As its little feet grazed my nose, I chuckled from the ticklish sensation. "Well, I'm not afraid of you. I think you're a majestic being, too beautiful for this world."

The moth flipped over, its large wings flapping happily in the Spring air. I had a feeling my words meant a lot to it. Hell, maybe it felt the same way about me. I guess we were kindred spirits.

"You still haven't told me your name," I pointed out. "I take that as a sign that you don't have one?"

The moth squeaked once more, confirming my suspicions.

"Well, why don't we fix that?" I examined the bug in all its glory, admiring the grace it presented with as it fluttered. "Let's see. You are a gentle, misunderstood being that many people fear. But they shouldn't fear you, as your existence is just as normal as the air we breathe."

I smiled at my friend. "I know it's a scary name, but what about Death? Like you, people fear which they do not understand. I think it's safe to say death is something many people don't quite get."

The moth tilted a little onto its left side, watching me with an air of curiosity.

"I think it's fitting," I argued with a smile on my face. "Your skull pattern scares people, much like dead bodies scare people. But in ac-tuality, death isn't so scary at all. It's just the end of your current life and the start of another. Fresh slate! That sounds pretty sweet to me," I offered the little guy a wink. "Like you. You're pretty sweet."

My friend spun around in a little circle, wings flapping with friv-olous delight.

"So it's settled then. You're Death."

And just like that, Death flew off into the sky, disappearing behind a tall oak tree. "See you later," I called out. I looked down at my sandwich, realizing I only had one bite left before I was finished. And I didn't feel sick! Death certainly comforted me during my moment of weakness.

What a swell creature.

I would one day find out its gender.

That way I'd know how to appropriately approach it.

With that, I took the final bite of my lunch. I savored the spicy love affair between the turkey, swiss cheese, and seasoning. Rubbing my hands together, I spotted Maron in the distance, handing out flyers. Taking advantage, I stood up and jogged over towards her. "Hey girl!"

She looked up at me and smiled wide. "Hey Mel!"

I stopped in front of her and smiled. "What's new?"

"Eh," she said with a light shrug. "Not much. Work-study has me passing out flyers for some science presentation later tonight," She took a flyer and handed it over to me. "Here, take one."

I grabbed onto the piece of paper and examined the contents. "I thought advertisements were supposed to be flashy," I commented. "This is just a black question mark with a white background."

Maron squinted at me. "Did you even read the bold text?"

"I did," I said. "It says "Come see a world changing experiment for the ages--too rare for this world"," I held my hands up, giving Maron jazz hands. "Oooh. *Spooky.*"

The blonde sighed. "Yeah, it sounds hokey to me, too. But hey, I'm getting paid to hand these out, so I can't complain too much, you know?"

I shrugged. "I suppose that's true."

"You know," Maron said with a smile. "I get paid extra if I attend this presentation. Wanna give me some company while I suffer through this?"

I blew some air through my lips. The answer was going to be yes regardless, as I wanted to support my friend. But at the same time, I didn't want to waste my time on a presentation that was likely going to bore me to tears.

"Do I have to? Science isn't really my strong suit, so I'll be completely lost."

Maron puffed her bottom lip out. "*Please?* Pretty please? Don't make me suffer alone."

With a chuckle, I ran a hand through my hair. "Okay, fine. Just for you, though."

She grinned widely. "Awesome! See you tonight, then."

I cocked an eyebrow and looked back at the flyer. Sure enough, it said that the presentation was at eight o'clock that night. "Ah, dammit," I muttered under my breath.

| **six** |

A Saving Grace

Eight o'clock wasted no time in rearing its ugly head in my direction. What have I gotten myself into, I asked myself. Maron was my friend and all, but I had no business attending a science presentation. After the horrifyingly embarrassing show I'd put on in Dr. Barris's class, I just wanted to crawl under a rock and never leave.

What if I showed up and people started laughing at me?

What if they ridiculed me for being a fucking moron?

I knew Maron would've felt bad, had that been what happened.

Not looking to take any chances, I wore a green hoodie and kept my hood up so my face was mostly covered. I stuffed my hands into the front pocket and made my way to the auditorium. The place wasn't necessarily packed, needless to say. Maron certainly tried to pique people's interest, but only managed to enthrall a small handful of people.

Oh well.

Perhaps the lack of an audience would inspire the speakers to speed the presentation up so everyone could go to bed. As I stepped down to the first row, I spotted Maron and took my seat beside her. she looked over at me and giggled. "Chilly?"

I snorted. "Sure."

"C'mon, Melbourne," she cooed, grabbing my hood and pulling it down. "What are you going to lose by having your face seen at this event? Since when have you cared about reputation, anyway?"

With a hiss, I quickly grabbed my hood and pulled it back over my head. "Stop, Maron. I did something stupid and I don't want people seeing me."

She cocked an eyebrow. "Oh? Do tell."

"No," I said in a harsh whisper. "I can't. I won't. It hurts too much."

The blonde folded her arms. "C'mon, Mel. You know I'm not going to judge. What did you do that was so terrible?"

I bit my bottom lip. Did I dare tell her and risk my secret coming out? I had only just been diagnosed with a mental illness. I didn't want everyone and their mother knowing. Even though I trusted Maron, I didn't trust the prying ears of the ten other people in the auditorium.

I sighed.

I supposed I could tell her an abridged version.

"I gave an answer in class that was so braindead that my teacher thought I was a babbling idiot."

"How braindead are we talking?" Maron asked, prying for more information than I was willing to give. "Are we talking "flat earth"

braindead, or "whoopsie, I got a wrong answer and now I'm embarrassed" braindead?"

I glared at my friend. I knew what she was trying to do. She was
trying to help me recontextualize my shame. But it just wasn't going
to work on me. I had made such an unreasonably huge ass of myself
that I half-contemplated dropping out of the class and changing my
major. Perhaps creative writing? Literally anything that didn't involve
me showing my face, like programming?

"Teetering on "flat earth", girl."

Maron clenched her teeth and pulled the hood further down my
face. "You'll need this."

I snorted again. "I'm glad you understand."

After a couple minutes, the lights dimmed in the auditorium, only
for the lights upon the stage to luminate. In the corner of my eye, I
saw two guys in lab coats approaching the steps leading to the stage.
One looked like your stereotypical poindexter, black-rimmed glasses,
pimply face and all. The second was a rather short, but handsome man
with sandy blonde hair spiked up, which complimented his own pair
of black-rimmed glasses.

Once they made it to the center of the stage, they faced the small
audience. The poindexter threw his arms up. "Really?" he asked in a
deep voice. "This is all that decided to come? What the actual fu--"

"Now now," the blonde scientist said, patting his partner's shoulder. "Our flyers were admittedly cryptic. Everyone probably thinks
we're snake oil salesmen," he pointed at himself. "I would think the
same, truth be told. That's what I get hiring my twelve-year-old
brother to design the flyers."

His joke went unappreciated. The only reaction he got from us was a girl in the back clearing her throat. Even Maron and myself weren't amused by his feeble attempt to engage the crowd.

With a nervous chuckle, the handsome scientist adjusted his collar. "S-So anyway. Hello, everyone. I'm Filmore Baskin. You can call me Phil, though," he pointed at his partner. "This is Ian Derry. We were once students, just like you. Luckily, our alma mater agreed to let us set up shop in the science building. So you'll probably be seeing us a lot around here from now on!"

More crickets chirped as Ian cleared his throat. "We've called for this presentation today not because we're looking to bore you to tears--"

"Really?" heckled a guy in the back. "I never would've fucking guessed!"

"*Hey*," Phil shouted. "Get the hell out of our presentation if you have nothing nice to say!"

With an exaggerated sigh, the brunette poindexter ran his hands through his curly hair. The blonde growled as the door to the auditorium opened and promptly closed. "Anyone else want to leave? Miss out on this life-changing experiment because you have the patience of a petulant child?"

I attempted to stand up, but Maron pushed me back down into my seat. "Ugh, *fine!*" I exclaimed.

The two scientists glared daggers at the audience for a moment, waiting for more people to leave. When nobody else moved, Ian nodded slowly. "Right. Okay. So now we know who is dedicated to break-throughs in biochemistry."

Phil held up a finger. "Not only biochemistry, but also medical science. It's exactly what people have been begging for...dreaming of...since the beginning of time. We looked at each other and decided to make that dream a reality. Nobody else is willing to do it, so why not us?"

I cocked an eyebrow. The men's flyers weren't the only cryptic thing about the presentation. I had an odd feeling in the pit of my stomach about where it was going. Was it going to trigger some kind of beast within me, or was I just going to cry in absolute boredom?

"But we're getting ahead of ourselves, aren't we Phil?" Ian commented. "First, we need to explain just how we aim to make this dream a reality," he looked at the audience with a big smile on his face. "It all begins with genetic mutations..."

"Here we go," I droned, rolling my eyes. I attempted to stand up, but Maron stopped me again. 'C'mon, Maron. I need to pee."

She scowled at me. "No, you don't. Sit down."

With another groan, I reluctantly took my seat back. "If I piss my-self, I'm blaming you."

Now it was her turn to roll her eyes. "Shut up and listen to the pre-sentation."

I breathed through my nose as I continued to listen to the scientists babble on about molecules, drugs, and genetics. It seemed to take ages for any kind of point to be made. I certainly kept my eyes on the screen of my cell phone, counting down the minutes before I could go back to my dorm room and sleep.

A person could only suffer so long.

But, like dreams, the journey is often arduous before reaching the whimsical paradise that is the destination.

The journey spawned from within the minds of Ian and Phil were no different.

"But, we've explained too much," Phil commented. "For those of you who are still awake, congratulations! You've made it to the big reveal."

I folded my arms. "This should be good," I murmured.

"You see," Ian said with a grin. "We may just be two men, but we're building a company that will take the world by storm."

I groaned.

What company *didn't* mutter that phrase?

"Ladies and gentlemen," Phil announced. "We are Aeon Industries and we bring you *this*."

The blonde motioned for a stagehand to open the curtains, to which they dutifully followed their instructions. The red velvet curtains opened, revealing a brightly lit stage. Sitting solitary in the middle was a glass case. Inside the case was a metallic jug. Across the middle was a label reading "TerraCure."

"This is the TerraCure serum, folks," Phil happily announced. "Much like terraforming changes the landscape of the Earth, TerraCure changes the biological markers we possess."

Ian stepped ahead of Phil, smiling wide. "What we're saying, ladies and gentlemen, is that we can rewrite your entire genetic make-up. Change who you are as a person. New personality, an abundance of physical improvements, refined prowess in social situations, a better grasp at sexual intercourse...whatever you want to change, we can manage that!"

I chuckled nervously. "That is a scam," I muttered to Maron. Of course, just because the words left my mouth didn't mean that I actually believed them. I don't know how or why, but once they stopped with the science mumbo jumbo, I found myself enthralled with the idea of TerraCure.

My mental illness would be cured.

My inability to maintain some semblance of normalcy would be fixed.

Hell, maybe I'd become a gender I felt comfortable expressing!

"Does it sound like a pipe dream, folks?" Ian asked the half-awake audience. "It may sound like one, but it isn't. It's a reality. Or at least it will be, once we collect the sufficient amount of funds needed to perfect the serum."

"That's right, folks," Phil chimed in. "TerraCure is only in its beta form at the moment. It's been tested on particularly feral animals, changing their entire personality exponentially."

He flashed a smirk.

"Don't worry. It's one hundred percent pet-friendly."

The audience clearly wasn't buying into the talk of miracles. They looked ready to die at any moment. The scientists clearly noticed this, as they decided to wrap things up. "So yeah," muttered Phil. "If you're interested in helping us make this dream a reality, we'll be here for the next hour or two. Stop by and let's chat. Thank you."

At that moment, everyone stood up and began hauling ass for the exit. Maron stretched her arms at the conclusion of the presentation. "That was boring," she admitted once and for all. "But hey. It's extra pocket change."

I forced a grin. "Yeah. Fuck you for dragging me to this."

She took a playful bow. "I aim to please, m'lord."

As Maron turned around to grab her jacket from off the back of her chair, I caught sight of the two scientists exiting stage left. "Hey Maron," I said, putting on my trickster voice. "Dare me to go ask those guys about that serum?"

She turned to face me, glaring. "Don't you dare."

"Too late," I said before sticking my tongue out at my friend. "I'll be right back."

And so I trekked forward to find my saving grace, all under the guise of a joke.

| seven |

Viable Options

I approached Phil and Ian quickly once I noticed they were headed toward the front row seats of the auditorium. I had hoped Maron assumed I had simply wished to catch them before they got too far. I would've died if she figured out my true intentions. Maybe I was a fool for buying into their miracle work. Any normal person would've written the two goofs off as con artists and called it a day.

But unfortunately, I wasn't entirely convinced of their allegedly malicious scheme.

I was, for a lack of a better word, desperate for some kind of reprieve.

To be "normal" was a pipe dream in any other circumstance.

But not then.

So, under an admittedly weak guise, I rushed up to the two scientists. "Excuse me! Ian! Phil!" The latter had already taken his seat and the former was hovering over his own, mid-squat. They both looked my way with intrigue.

Once I reached them, I flashed them a partially authentic smile. "Hey guys. How are you doing?" The two men stared at me, not uttering a single word. Already thrown off, I awkwardly cleared my throat. "I-uh-I had questions about TerraCure."

Ian nodded and Phil pushed his glasses up the bridge of his nose. "Ask away," the handsome scientist instructed. "We're happy to assist anyway we can."

With a slow nod, I turned my head to see if Maron was listening in. To my relief, she was not; she was scrolling on her phone. With a quick sigh, I turned my head to look at the two men. "I, um, am interested in your product--uh, obviously, of course. I was wondering if..." I took a deep breath, bracing myself for the worst. "I was wondering if TerraCure can cure, like, mental illness?"

The poindexter nodded slowly. "Of course. If it can fix genetics, the neurons in the human brain would be a no-brainer."

Phil smirked. "Depression and anxiety are super easy to treat even without TerraCure, so of course."

I cleared my throat. "I, um, was actually thinking something more intense. Like schizoaffective disorder? More specifically the bipolar variant?"

The handsome scientist's eyes widened. "Oh. Now that's an interesting idea. Treating severe mental illness would be an excellent way to showcase the serum's potential."

I smiled legitimately, starting to feel a little more at ease. "R-Right! If it can, then I will purchase your serum in a heartbeat!"

Ian stood up and patted imaginary dust off his thighs. "Come to think of it, we've never tested the serum on a human test subject before. If you, Mister..."

"Melbourne," I answered, ignoring the misgendering for the sake of recovery.

The scientist nodded slowly. "Melbourne. Interesting name," he cleared his throat. "If you were interested in maybe being our first human subject, we'd pay you an exorbitant sum."

I bit my bottom lip for the sake of quelling an incoming squeal. "Sign me up! I'm available anytime! When do I need to be in your lab?!"

Phil chuckled from his seat. "Slow down there, man. We still need funds of our own before we can afford to conduct any actual clinical trials."

"H-How much do you need?" I asked, visibly shaking with anticipation. "I can fundraise for you guys!"

The two men looked at each other, smirking at one another. Ian then looked back my way. "Half a million."

My jaw dropped. "I'm sorry, what?"

"It's true," Phil said with an obviously faux sigh. "In order for us to produce enough of the serum to support a human being, we need an unreasonably high surplus of ingredients to break down into concocting the product. That will be extremely expensive."

I blinked rapidly a few times. "I think you guys are pulling my leg and just trying to squeeze as much money out of a mere college student as possible."

Phil shrugged. "It's not our fault that science is expensive. Perhaps if your schizoaffective disorder is such a plight in your life, you'd have no qualms about helping us out?"

I shook my head slowly. "I-It *is* a major plight in my life. But I don't have the confidence to raise half a million bucks for you guys."

"I mean," Ian piped up. "Maybe more people will be willing to donate to our cause. If so, then you wouldn't have to raise so much money. Worst case scenario, we rescind the monetary offer and just take you in as an unpaid test subject."

"Even then," Phil added. "We still need money to make the serum. No way around that, I'm afraid."

I swallowed hard. There was no chance in hell anyone but me would take them seriously enough to give them money. "I...will do what I can."

The two men clapped their hands together. "Excellent! We look forward to seeing what you come up with."

With one last reluctant nod, I turned away from them and made my way back towards my best friend. Half a million dollars was an impossible goal. But goddammit, I wanted to be normal. Just one day of normalcy would've been enough to lift my spirits.

I would return to Maron the ever pleasing jester. But behind closed doors, I would be plotting. TerraCure would be my saving grace. I wasn't going to let such an opportunity pass me by.

| eight |

Discreet Scheming

The next morning, class presented as far less humiliating. A few of my peers gave me discerning looks, but didn't wish to poke the bear. I could go on about how much of a relief it was, but that would've been a waste of time. I didn't have time to relish in the opinions of others or even the subtlety of their wandering eyes.

Truth be told, I needed a plan.

I needed to be fixed.

I needed to be set free.

But how could a lowly college student such as myself possibly help raise half a million dollars? I didn't have a job, nor did I have time to acquire one. After all, class was grueling and demanded much of my attention. And I wasn't rich by any means, so I couldn't rely on a trust fund to pay the way.

So what could I do?

Dr. Barris began the lesson as usual, but I paid no mind to him. I might've been watching him, but it was a stretch to say I was absorbing the information he was feeding us. He didn't even approach me before class to check in on me. I sort of bolted from his classroom in a moment of humiliation; one would think a professor who loved his job would have the tact to ask a troubled student if they were okay. I guess it was my bad to assume that he enjoyed his work or valued his students.

Besides, I had more important things on my mind. Rather than jotting down notes from the lesson, I used my pencil to record the racing thoughts in my head. If the piece of paper wasn't sufficient enough to handle my thinking, then I'd get another sheet. And another. And maybe one more, for extra measure.

The first line read "ideas" and nothing more. Down beneath were three bullet points, accompanied by blankness beside each. I stared at the page, a million thoughts racing through my head; not one involving a decent idea. "Shit," I mouthed under my breath.

I was at a complete stand-still.

I hadn't the slightest inkling of what to do.

With a quiet shrug, I wrote down the words "antiques", "cards", and "sex". What did these words all have in common? The answer was simple, really. They were all things that could be sold.

My folks held on to a lot of old junk from back when my dad was growing up. My grandparents grew up in England and moved to the United States upon getting married. They brought all sorts of trinkets from the UK. They brought paperweights, fine china, silverware, and an old grandfather clock that, if I were to bring it to a shop, would probably start working again.

Dad found novelty in these items due to them being "delightfully British". I hadn't the heart to tell him that almost everything and everyone in the United States was British. Oh well, I thought to my-self. I was sure he'd either find out one day, or die an ignorant, happy old man.

With cards, I had a whole bunch of Pokemon trading cards from when I was a kid. I was a few generations behind, but I collected my fair share; at least three hundred cards. That would've colored anyone impressed, I believed. Surely I could've made a pretty penny selling them to a bigger enthusiast than myself.

As for sex, well...I didn't think I needed to elaborate on that.

I wasn't exactly pretty, but surely any desperate John or Jane would be willing to give me a try.

I sighed, quickly thinking of scenarios in which my ideas would fail. "Fuck." I lowered my head onto the table as frustration began to sink in.

Perhaps I could've held out hope that some rich kid would fund TerraCure for me? Everybody had flaws; flaws that I was sure they'd prefer to be without. With a quick shrug, I jotted the phrase "trust fund baby" onto the piece of paper.

Alas, I once again began thinking of ways in which the plan would fail. What if those people had no desire in TerraCure? What if they thought themselves perfect? I understood that the one-percent were snobby narcissists, but surely their own vanity would lure them into the open embrace of Aeon Industries, right? Everyone had their dirty little secrets.

I leaned back in my chair, looking up at the disgruntled professor with a convincing gaze. I might've been watching him, but my eyes felt like they belonged to a doll; plastic and colored with acrylic paint.

If there were only one human being in the history of ever to have mastered the art of looking without seeing, it would've been me.

Of course, that didn't mean nothing had trespassed into my vision, for a familiar entity had surfaced before me. Raising its little head up from behind Dr. Barris's desk, the beautiful creature known as Death looked straight at me. In my lack of conscious sight, I was able to zone in on the moth fairly quickly. I smiled at my friend and offered a discreet wave.

This appeased the insect, as it then fluttered its wings and rose up. As it hovered over the desk, I took a quick glance around. Nobody seemed to notice Death's sudden appearance. That potentially could've been a bad thing for me, as I had been diligently taking my medications every day since being discharged from Fairfield.

Or perhaps it wasn't madness at all.

Maybe I was chosen to receive some kind of special message.

Perhaps my little friend was an angel sent from the astral plane.

Choosing to give in to what my eyes were witnessing, I watched the moth flap its large wings over to the classroom door. Landing onto the brass door handle, it stepped a little to its left so it could look me in the eyes. I looked at Death quizzically. "*Open?*" I mouthed.

The moth gave its wings a quick flap, telling me that I had assumed its intentions correctly. It wanted to leave Dr. Barris's boring class as much as I did. I would've been sure to give it what we both wanted. The question was how. How could I escape without raising too much suspicion?

Dare I raise my hand and ask to be excused?

Dare I find a way to distract the professor long enough to escape?

Dare I enlist Maron's help in getting me out of class?

She was just a text away, after all.

My hand reached into my hoodie pocket, fingers sliding over the back of my phone. My eyes kept shifting between Death's fruitless efforts in leaving the classroom and Dr. Barris's constant pacing. I could've quickly whipped out the cellular device and shot a quick text to my best friend while his back was turned. He'd be none the wiser, as he seemed too focused on synapses and neurons to notice my shift movements.

Then, a thought crossed my mind. What if Maron wasn't paying attention to her phone? What if she had no signal? What if it was dead?

I eyeballed my delicate moth friend once more, noticing its urgency in escaping the psychology professor's domain. I decided at that moment that I could not wait for Maron's response. There were some things she could not have possibly understood, even if she attempted to level with me and see things from my point of view.

So, for Death's sake, I quickly stood up from my seat, pushing my chair back a couple inches. "I gotta go."

Dr. Barris stopped talking mid-sentence and glanced over at me. "Melbourne, what are you--"

Wasting no time, I rushed for the door. Death quickly fluttered upward so I could turn the handle without hurting it. Once the door was open, the moth and I both darted outside into the hallway.

As the door closed behind us, I glanced up at the insect. It had its back turned to me, the skull staring straight at me. "Is everything okay, friend?"

Death out a little squeak and flew away from me. It was not trying to leave me, however. I could tell by how slowly it moved. Something had spooked the moth, and it beckoned me to escort it to another location.

Death paved a new path ahead.

I followed.

| nine |

Walking Nightmare

I began to step forward as the moth guided me. Like before, nobody had bothered to follow me outside the classroom. Nobody seemed to care that I had made another exaggerated exit in two days.

I knew well that people would start getting sick of it.

They'd send school officials to give me another maliciously coordinated "wellness check".

I might've even been hospitalized again.

None of that mattered to me at the moment. It was no coincidence that Death had appeared when it did. In my time of need, I needed a guiding hand. I needed to be pointed in the right direction. The moth knew this.

And so I followed the insect toward the restrooms. Likely aware of society's generally malevolent view of people who dance on the gender spectrum, Death landed on the door to the men's room, just a couple inches above the metallic door handle. I nodded at the insect. "Smart cookie, you are." Taking the hint, I grabbed the handle and opened the door.

The unpleasant smell of hot farts and vomit wafted into my nostrils. Within a few steps into the restroom, I found myself holding my hand over my mouth. I gagged as I stepped into the direction Death was leading toward; a mirror over one of the four sinks. The moth gently landed onto the glass and let out another squeak.

"Is that what you wanted me to see, Death?"

The moth squeaked once more.

"It's a mirror, "I explained to the insect. "It shows your reflection," I poked my index finger into the glass. "See that gorgeous bug right there? That's you."

With another quick squeak, the moth stepped upward over the mirror. My eyes followed the insect until I finally gave in to the curious urge to look at my own reflection. To no surprise, I looked disheveled. My hair was a mess, and sagging bags rested under my eyes. Much to my horror, it appeared I was growing my facial hair back, as well.

"You're lucky, my friend," I commented as I ran a hand through my hair. "You're so beautiful and majestic. I look like a slob."

Death responded with a defiant squeak.

"It's true, though," I argued. "You may not see it yourself, but I certainly do."

The moth tapped its front feet against the glass. I had hoped that it would've been observing its form in the mirror, acknowledging my words as a possible fact. It didn't take beauty to know beauty, and I needed this little creature to know its worth in the world; if not the whole world, but my own.

"I've told you before," I said calmly. "I'm not afraid of you. The big skull on your back doesn't bother me. I've seen campy horror movies with scarier sights."

Death lifted its feet away from the mirror and hovered upward. Before I could say much else, the insect flew up to my face. I jumped back a little, startled by the sudden closeness. The moth then gently landed atop my forehead.

"H-Hey. What're you..."

The beautiful bug slowly walked up my head, its little feet stepping between my hairs. Once it was directly on top of my skull, the insect turned to face the mirror again as it nestled comfortably on my scalp. I couldn't speak moth, unfortunately. However, I had an inkling on what message Death was trying to purvey.

"*You're beautiful, too,*" the moth was probably thinking. "*You need to give yourself more credit towards your own beauty.*"

With a deep sigh, I shook my head. "I can't possibly agree with that. Nothing is even remotely enticing about me, Death. Just look at me. Take a really, *really* good look at me and tell me what exactly you find so beautiful about me."

The moth did not respond to me. No more sudden movements, no more squeaking. I gave the bug a small shrug. It couldn't argue with my logic, it seemed. I knew I was right.

"See? I told you there's no--"

Before I could finish my thought, another sight caught my attention. It was something so fast that I swore I had just blinked too hard.

My eyes were clearly playing tricks on me. It wouldn't be the first time that's happened to me and it certainly wouldn't be the last; not by a long shot.

But then the sight appeared again, this time lingering a little longer than before. The image in particular rested between my eyes, barely covered up by my wispy bangs. From a quick glance over, it looked like static rumbling in my forehead. Before I could get a long enough look, the sight vanished.

"Huh," I muttered. "For a second, it seemed like--"

As the static appeared once more, I took the opportunity to sweep my hair aside in order to get a closer look of what was going on with my skin. As I suspected, there was definitely some movement going on under my flesh. The longer I looked at the spot, it began to look more like a circle of tiny worms crawling around. I squinted at my reflection, eyes fixated on the odd spot.

"What the--"

Much to my horror, the worms began to poke up, testing the elasticity of my skin. As my eyes widened, I felt my breath hitch as one worm in particular started to rise up a little higher than the rest. "*Holy fuck*," I muttered shakily. "What the fuck is this?!"

I gasped loudly as the worm finally managed to poke a hole in my head. A pink worm, no longer than a centimeter, began inching out of my forehead. The bug wasn't able to move very far until it fell down into the sink.

As I glanced down at the fallen bug, my attention almost immediately returned to my forehead. Another worm began to poke out of my body, adjacent to the original hole. A second worm slithered outward and met the same fate as the first. "No," I breathed in a quiet panic. "*No!*"

Soon, two more worms forced their way out of my forehead before falling into the white porcelain sink. Then two more, and then two more after that. "How many of you are there?!"

Suddenly, the weak flap of flesh within the circle tore open. The floodgates unleashed, as a bunch of tiny pink worms tumbled out of my forehead and revealed the red inner layer of tissue protecting my skull. I tried to scream, but the muscles in my throat constricted. And just as I thought the worst had already come to pass, another bombshell dropped onto my head like an anchor hitting the seabed.

Something began to pull the tissue apart inside my head, blood running down my face like wet paint freshly applied to drywall. I covered my mouth with my hands, hoping the lack of support would hide the horrific sight behind my bangs. Alas, the growing entity inside my head was applying too much force for it to be simply hidden on its own.

That's precisely what this thing wanted.

It wanted to be seen.

And it wanted to see me.

An eyeball matching my own opened wide inside the crevice within my forehead. It blinked rapidly as I quivered with fear. I was unable to speak, so all I could do was look upward at the top of my head, above the offending spot. Death remained atop my scalp.

I quietly begged the moth to make it all end.

If only I could've verbalized my discomfort with the entire situation, then maybe the madness would've ended before it got as far as it did.

But I couldn't speak.

I couldn't utter a single word.

Tears began to form in my eye sockets as my teeth bore down on my bottom lip. This was more than I ever wanted to see. Of all the perceived atrocities I had ever laid my eyes on, it was certainly the worst at that point in my life.

But suddenly, the eyeball closed.

The hole sealed itself shut.

And before I knew it, the horrors occurring on my skin had come to an end.

With the realization that my mind's evil had finished having its fun, the muscles in my throat began to loosen and my breathing began to reactivate. My hands slowly dragged down my torso, my mouth wide open in shock. "Wha...*what?!*"

As I had finally gained the ability to verbalize my thoughts, the moth atop of my head lifted upward and flew away toward the stalls behind me. "Wait, friend?!" But Death had left me for the time being. I was left alone once again with my panic and racing thoughts. What I would've given to be able to comprehend moth language. What was the insect trying to tell me? What did it have to gain from making me witness such body horror?

Was it to prove a point?

Was it to teach me a lesson?

If anything, it really only made one thing clear to me at that moment in time; I needed TerraCure more than I first realized. My psychosis was getting worse the longer I went without it. All of the ideas I had to fix this issue were beginning to sound equally appetizing.

Selling antiques.

Selling Pokemon cards.

Selling sex.

Selling kiss-assery to some rich kid.

Everything sounded like a good idea for that damn serum. Shit, I'd even give something very outlandish a try; such as opening a fundraiser. Even if I needed to bite the bullet and find a part-time job, I would do that as well; my studies be damned.

Death's message had become as clear as day. If I really wanted to make the change, I needed to fight tooth and nail for it. I needed to personally ensure that Aeon Industries succeeded in funding their research. I was far too imperfect to function in society. I needed to square up, lest I fell down a deep pit of obscurity and disappointment.

"Thank you, friend," I muttered, shivering from the residue shock of what I'd seen.

| ten |

Going Once, Going Twice

One look back into my trunk would've possibly saved me from getting an ear-chewing from my folks. But once one made the commitment to packing their car up full of expensive junk, the only option at that point was to sell it to whatever card shop or pawn shop they could come across. That was certainly my plan. I made a mad dash home after I'd seen such visceral horrors in the men's restroom outside my classroom. My family was out, so I didn't have to answer any questions as I raided the garage.

I stocked up fast and made a run for it. Worst case scenario, I sold everything and offered to give Dad a fair percentage. Of course, I would've rather not done that at all. I needed the money more than I needed his understanding. Or perhaps I wouldn't sell anything at all, which would probably please him greatly. However, I would be distraught.

So, in my rush to get away with murder, I sped off to my first destination; the local card and comic shop. I hadn't been there before, as I hadn't really paid any mind to my Pokemon collection since I was a kid. While it would've made more sense to deal with the heavier merchandise first, the card shop just happened to be within my reach sooner. Plus, I still hadn't committed to selling my antiques at a pawn shop, or an antique shop. I was sure the antique shop would've been the safer bet, but I hadn't really spent much time scoping such places out. Antiques were more my father's thing, after all.

As I pulled up into the parking lot, I noticed right off the bat that there were quite a few customers occupying space. This was good, I thought to myself. I had a great opportunity to make some big bucks. And considering I had up to the fourth generation of cards, I was sure to make bank with the fellow nerds.

I parked my rust bucket and wasted no time grabbing my bin from the backseat of my car. The entire thing was full of valuable pieces of cardboard. If I wasn't able to make a profit from this venture, then TerraCure was surely out of my grasp.

The shop was packed wall-to-wall with customers looming over glass counters. Some held bins as big, or bigger, than mine. I either chose the best time to sell my cards, or the worst. Either way, I knew I needed to get busy working my magic; whatever magic I might've had, anyway.

"'Scuse me," I muttered repeatedly as I maneuvered through the crowded store. The walls were decorated in bright colors, advertising recently released comics and graphic novels. I had always wanted to get into comics, but I just couldn't ever bring myself to sit down long enough to get invested into a neverending story. Reading was rewarding, but I suppose it took a very special kind of story to get my blood pumping.

Alas, that seemed to be the nature of my mental illness.

My interests seemed to be feigned for the sake of everyone else.

No passion, no focus.

I just wanted to feel better.

I had almost made it to the front counter before an overweight dude wearing a Digimon t-shirt cut in front of me, knocking me backwards. Tumbling over, I desperately clutched onto the bin's handles. I was not looking forward to having to fight the horde over my merchandise. We weren't a bunch of pigeons fighting over scraps.

"Dude," I crowed loudly. "Can you watch where you're going?"

Alas, he did not hear me. The surrounding noise canceled out my complaint, my voice whisked away into the ether like a forgotten thought. Maybe it was for the best, I told myself. No need to get into a fight with a guy who will forget about me within the next half-hour.

At least, that was my initial thought.

Once I regained my composure, I straightened up my posture and shuffled up to the counter. As I readied myself to set the bin onto the surface, the asshole in the Digimon shirt struck again. This time, he slapped a bunch of comic books onto the countertop. He was rank with the smell of sweat and unclean rectal cavities. His own body odor was permeating throughout the store, enhancing the fragrance of the surrounding customers, who were equally sweaty.

To say I was feeling nauseated was an understatement.

"Ay Bobby!" the customer roared hoarsely. "Can I get my discount on these bad boys?"

The dark-skinned cashier with a small afro picked up two comic books from his stack and examined the front covers. "Bro, these just came out yesterday. What discount are you talking about?"

The sweaty man let out an obnoxious cackle. "The new merchandise discount, *obviously*! Todd Franks has been hyping his release for months now, and Harry Taylor just announced the release of "Ravenous Witches" on his Twitter page. Sounds like first dibs to me, man.

The cashier, Bobby, snorted. "The only deals we have for new comics are for customers who pre-ordered. They usually get a thirty percent discount."

"Right," the man responded, clearly not registering the information he was being told. "That's what I'm saying! I get a thirty percent discount."

Bobby and I made eye contact, exchanging equal looks of exasperation. "Dude," the cashier sighed. "You didn't pre-order the latest issue of "Ravenous Witches". You didn't pre-order the latest issue of "Steel Fist", either. You have to pay the full price."

Distraught over the bad news, the man in the Digimon shirt started flailing his arms like a spastic child. "Check your computer! It's *there*! My name is in the system!"

I rolled my eyes before ultimately succumbing to the weight of my bin. I dropped my cards by my feet and crossed my arms. "Can you hurry this up, please? I have places I need to be."

The customer waved me off, keeping his eyes on the cashier. "Check the computer. Now. I want my discount."

I was losing my patience quickly. Where the hell did this guy get off trying to boss people around? He didn't work there, nor did he seem to be a supplier of any sort. He possessed an attitude as foul as his body odor and everyone's lives would've been better if he had left the property.

"Hey *asshole*," I shouted over the crowd. "Either buy something or get the fuck out of here."

Finally, the jerk looked at me. "Buzz off, fresh meat. This ain't got nothing to do with you."

"I want to be able to leave this store before I go gray in the hair," I snapped. "*Get out.* I have shit I need to sell and you're wasting my time."

He looked down at my feet, taking notice of my bin full of Pokemon cards. "This yours?"

"Yeah," I nodded. "It's mine."

The asshole customer snorted. "Impressive collection, I guess. Are they all first edition?"

I rubbed the back of my head. "Are they original, you mean?"

"Yeah," he clarified. "You ain't gonna sell shit if they're all reprints."

I felt a weight being lifted from my lungs, a sense of cautious comfort overtaking me. "I've been collecting these since I was a kid. I know the third and fourth gens are original. I'm pretty sure the first and second gens are, too."

"Bullshit," he coughed. "First edition came out in 1999. You look like you're a college baby. Guaranteed your first gens are reprints. Probably your second gens, too."

I cleared my throat. "So what? Even if they are reprints, there's still value in them. And my third and fourth gens are absolutely original. I fucking bought them with my allowance when I was a kid!"

At that point, the asshole flashed me a shit-eating grin. "Keep telling yourself that, kid. Now why don't you beat it? I got a discount to cash in on."

He turned away from me, but I wasn't having it. The fucking nerve of this guy! He didn't have x-ray vision! He couldn't tell if my merchandise was legitimate or not! I wasn't going to let him convince Bobby to turn me away just because of a hunch!

I lobbed a closed fist into his neck, striking him like a venomous snake. He instantly toppled over onto the counter. Much to my horror, his body weight was enough to crush the display case beneath his stack of unpaid comicbooks. Bobby jumped back in shock as the glass shattered.

Fuck.

Fuck!

"*God fucking dammit,*" I wailed in a desperate panic. "I'm sorry. I'm so fucking sorry. Oh my God."

Knowing well that I had just hammered the nails into my own coffin, I picked up my bin and made my move for the door. Customers oohed and ahhed over the drama before them. A few guys patted me on the back. A couple of them told me "good job".

Good jobs don't result in destroyed property.

That wasn't a good job.

Not by a long shot.

| eleven |

A Tinkerer's Dilemma

With one venture thrown out the window, it was time to go with my Plan B. True, there was no shortage of stores I could've visited with the intention of selling my Pokemon cards. However, word spreads fast. I was sure that I was officially blacklisted from any and all comic shops in town.

Thankfully, my school had a computer lab. With some research and dedication, I could've listed my merchandise online. Of course, it would've taken more time than I cared to spend. I supposed I had no choice in the matter.

"Dammit," I muttered under my breath as I drove a couple miles down the road to the nearest antique shop. "Dammit, dammit, dammit."

Desperation was hitting me hard. Why? It wasn't like there was a deadline in helping Aeon Industries raise money for TerraCure. The world wouldn't explode if I didn't manage to make enough money to fund the project, right?

I wasn't going to die or anything, or so I hoped.

As I drove down the empty street, a pink fairy materialized within my peripheral vision. She danced gracefully, her tip-toes guiding her body like easy ocean waves. Her dance was majestic, but I didn't understand why I was seeing her. What was she trying to tell me?

"You're beautiful," I mused, my eyes slowly drifting toward the creature. "But I'm afraid I don't understand why you're here."

The fairy's posture straightened upward and she took a bow.

"You're a wonderful dancer," I commented truthfully. "I wish I could do that."

She giggled, blushing brightly.

"I'm serious," I said, now placing my full focus on the lovely little pixie. "Life would be so much easier if I had just the smallest sliver of talent," with a forlorn sigh, I blinked slowly. "If I were good at something, the pain of living would be so much more manageable. I could temporarily forget about my problems and sink myself into a passion or two."

The fairy frowned and folded her arms.

"Consider yourself blessed," I continued. "You're able to live freely with no restrictions. The very fact that I see you at all just confirms that I'm trapped within the warped walls of my mind."

She scoffed, her face swelling with frustration.

"Don't be like that," I commented. "I'm not saying I hate seeing you. All I'm saying is just that I'm--"

Against my better judgement, I allowed myself to stray from the road's allure for one moment too long. Before it hit me, the front end of my car crashed headfirst into a bus stop bench. The impact jolted me forward, slamming me against the steering wheel. "*Fuck!*" I exclaimed, my heart practically leaping out of my throat.

I gasped repeatedly, hyperventilating from the realization of what had just happened. I had gotten into a car accident. My inability to maintain proper focus on my driving resulted in the unceremonious damaging of my car; my car that my father had been helping me make payments on. And once the airbag popped into my face, I knew it was all over for me.

The car was totaled.

Ten grand down the toilet.

My loss of a much-required form of transportation.

The inevitable invention from insurance and Dad.

The unspeakable horrors that would follow.

Once the surging pain in my face began to wane, I pulled away from the deployed airbag. Blood was smeared over the cloth, likely from my nose or mouth. Tears began to form in my eyes. "This can't be happening to me. It just can't!"

I quickly leaned forward, past the airbag. People were staring at me, eyes wide and mouths agape. Judging by the dirty clothing worn by the witnesses, I assumed they were homeless. One woman, tan-skinned with matted hair, clutched onto a blue and green quilt like it was her sole source of comfort in the dark, cold world.

Much to my relief, there didn't appear to be any casualties or injured victims; just a couple of concerned bystanders who wanted to catch the next bus. "Are you okay, sir?" asked a dark-skinned man with a crutch and blue bandana on his head. "You hurt? Need me to call 911?"

I frantically shook my head. "N-No! No need! I'm fine! Just startled!"

The man limped over to the driver's side of my car and motioned for me to lower my window. I did as I was told, coughing as I did it. "I-I'm okay, man. Really! I'm just really upset is all!"

"You're bleeding," he commented. "Imma need to call somebody. Make sure you ain't too bad off."

I choked on an incoming breath. "You don't need to do that. Please. It's already bad enough that this happened. I don't want any medical bills to be sent to my parents!"

"Well, you ain't got much of a choice, son," crowed an elderly black lady with an oversized t-shirt with sweat stains in the pits. "'Cuz the cops are already on their way. Probably some paramedics, too," she crossed her arms and shook her head. "This is why you don't drink and drive."

My eyes widened a little as a nervous chuckle left my mouth. "I-I haven't been drinking, ma'am. I'm just..."

I stammered over my next words.

What could I say?

Did I tell the truth and risk getting sent back to the psych ward?

Did I lie and say that I was sleep deprived?

Or could I perhaps place the blame on the car?

It wasn't my fault.

The car had a mind of its own!

"M-My power-steering clamped up on me," I said. "I tried to jerk it back, but I was too late."

She stared holes through me.

She clearly wasn't buying what I was selling.

"You have to believe me!" I pleaded. "I don't drink and drive! That's not a thing I do!"

"Boy, you best hope you don't blow nuthin' on that breathalyzer," murmured the man with the crutch. "Those cops would eat a kid like you alive."

Another breath got caught in my throat as the tell-tale sound of EMS sirens blared nearby. Soon after, two police cruisers pulled up beside me. Flashes of red and blue stabbed my retinas like sewing needles. I leaned back in my seat, closing my eyes tightly.

Maybe I'd find myself lying in bed momentarily.

Maybe all of this would've been a terrible nightmare that I addressed in therapy.

A rotund officer stepped out of one of the cruisers. He looked pretty much like a standard cop; bald, clean-shaven, Caucasian, and sporting aviator glasses. He stepped over my way, stopping at my open window. "Hello, son. I'm Officer Kipslinger. Are you injured?"

I shook my head. "No, sir. Just a bloody face and frayed nerves."

The officer gave a half nod. "I'd say so. May I see your license and registration, please?"

With a quick nod, I leaned over and opened my glove compartment. However, once opened, my eyes widened. If getting into a car accident because of a hallucination wasn't bad enough, it appeared I was going to have to juggle the attention of cops and the attention of an old man's face.

"*What are you doing, Melbourne?*" the face asked hoarsely. "*Why has this happened?*'

I swallowed.

"Is everything okay, sir?" Officer Kipslinger asked, maintaining a calm, professional tone of voice. "Is your registration in the vehicle?"

I nodded quickly. "Y-Yes. Give me a moment."

With a rapid breath, I shoved my hand into the face's cheek. His flesh was warm and moist, like he'd been lightly sweating. His eyes widened and he groaned as I felt around for any sign of perceptual reality. "*Is that really necessary, Melbourne?*"

Growing ever more frantic, I began to hyperventilate again as I flailed my hand in the glove compartment, slapping the man repeatedly.

"Easy, son," the policeman said with a quick breath. "It's okay. We're gonna get through this, okay?"

Tears returned to my eye sockets as I finally found the slip of paper. Despite my small victory, the sadness slipped away and wetted my cheeks. "G-Got it."

I handed the cop the registration, quickly realizing that I still needed to provide my license. With viscerally shaky hands, I pulled my black aniline wallet from out of my jacket pocket and handed it to Officer Kipslinger. "H-Here y-you go."

The heavy-set man took the wallet, but did not take his eyes off me. "Have you been drinking today?"

My face broke into a cold sweat. My skin felt clammy as my focus returned to the old man in my glove compartment. He looked at me with a flat, stony stare. He reminded me of a disappointed parent. "*You're better than this, you know.*"

I bit my lip. "N-No, officer. I h-haven't been drinking."

"*Look at yourself,*" the face commanded. "*You're making a fool out of yourself, and for what? What exactly are you hoping to accomplish here?*"

"Sir, I'll need you to step out of the vehicle," the officer instructed. "I just need to make sure you aren't driving under the influence."

My breathing was hard and fast. My heartbeat like a drum inside my chest. He was going to find something, I worried. Not alcohol. Not cannabis. Not even hard drugs. Just lots of insanity.

This is it; I told myself.

It was back to Fairfield Behavioral Hospital for me.

Two hospitalizations in less than a week.

Was I truly beyond repair?

"C'mon, sir," the cop urged. "Step out of the vehicle."

I looked at the old man in my glove compartment, he nodded his head toward the officer. "*He doesn't have all day, you know.*"

I swallowed hard and unbuckled my seatbelt. I slowly opened the door, hesitating to step out of my car. If I did, things would only get worse. If I didn't, things would only get worse. It was a no-win situation.

With a deep breath, I did as I was told and stepped out of the burgundy, 2015 Toyota Corolla. Once my feet were on the ground, I pushed myself up and reached behind me to close the door. As it shut, I looked up at the officer. "O-Okay. D-Do I need to blow into a breathalyzer or something?"

With a quick nod, Officer Kipslinger turned around and walked back to his cruiser. I watched him, conscious of every movement I made. Body language flowed like literature. Once someone watched you long enough, they could tell you every little thought circling around your brain.

I wanted to be as solid as an anchor.

Impenetrable.

Heavy.

Capable of supporting even the most stalwart ships.

The cop briefly popped his head and arms into the car, retracting once he had found what he was looking for. He headed back my way, holding up the device. "Okay, son. I'm going to hold this up to your mouth. I'll need you to wrap your lips around the tube and blow."

I released the breath building up within my lungs. "Okay. I'm ready."

The cop did precisely what he said he'd do. Once the breathalyzer was close enough to my face, I took the opaque white tube into my mouth. Without further hesitation, I blew into the device for a few seconds. Officer Kipslinger clicked a red button and pulled the device away.

"Huh. Nothing."

I stared blankly at the officer. "L-Like I said, officer. I haven't been drinking."

"Then what exactly caused this accident to happen, Mister..."

"Melbourne," I answered quickly. "Melbourne Thompson," I looked down at my feet and, much to my horror, the old man had returned. His face was now stuck to the ground, his judging eyes scanning me thoroughly.

"*Well? We're waiting.*"

I bit my lip and blurted out a question that defied what I truly wanted to say. "What do you want from me?"

I wasn't looking at Officer Kipslinger, but my third eye could see him as plain as day. His eyebrows rose, confusion chiseling itself into his slightly wrinkled face. "I'm sorry? What was that?"

As much as I wanted to backtrack with the policeman, I admittedly wanted to hear the old man's answer more. He glared at me, his wrinkles barely moving as he curled his lips into a deceiving smirk. The man looked to be ancient, possibly hundreds of years under his belt.

I thought for a moment that he was God.

I thought it was some kind of divine message from Heaven.

Thankfully, my assumption wasn't far off.

"You do realize that your fate is malleable, right?" he began to explain. *"One little decision can set the stage for things to come. The smallest little action may seem inconsequential to you now, but you'll find that it will open doors that might've not been accessible before,"* he closed his eyes. *"But it could also close doors you always thought would be open."*

"Sir?" Officer Kipslinger asked. "I asked you a question. What happened to cause this crash to happen?"

The homeless crowd, who were still present, began talking to him. However, I wasn't registering what was being said. I assumed they were telling him the story I had fed them. I just didn't care for the time being.

Why was this man telling me about fate?

It wasn't even a new lesson to be learned.

Everyone and their mother understood that the future depended on actions committed in the present.

What was even the point he was trying to make?

"You are the tinkerer of your existence, Melbourne," he continued. *"I have seen many a man give in to his own impulses. I have seen many a woman ruin their lives because of one negative interaction with another,"* his gaze softened. *"I know you are imperfect. You know it, too."*

I nodded. The people nearby didn't seem to notice, as they were still speaking amongst each other. "What are you trying to say?" I mouthed.

The old man stared at me, expression unchanging. *"Everything I have said reflects the truth, Melbourne. Be mindful of how easy things can change; whether or not it's for the best is up in the air."*

And just like that, the old man disappeared, evaporating into dust. He might've been gone, but his words lingered in my mind. Was he referring to my decision to utilize the services of Aeon Industries? I couldn't imagine he was talking about anything but TerraCure. Even with this thought in mind, I felt more dedicated to getting that serum than ever before.

Gone would be the hallucinations.

Gone would be disorganized thought content.

Gone would be the depression.

Gone would be Melbourne Thompson as they were born.

Arising from the ashes would be a phoenix, flying so high into the sky that the human couldn't even begin to keep up.

| twelve |

Come to Jesus

"What the fuck were you thinking, Melbourne? Really, what the actual fuck?"

My father's voice echoed off the hallway walls. Officer Kipslinger had called them on my behalf, explaining to them what had happened. They made short work of the roads between them and I before they picked me up and sped back home. Him and Mom were deathly silent for the entirety of the drive, occasionally looking up at the rearview mirror to stab me with their piercing eyes. Once we made it home, the screaming began.

"You're full of shit, kid," Dad continued, his face quickly turning beet red. "I literally just had the power-steering fluid changed in that car! I had its oil changed--its tires rotated! You have *any* idea how much money I've wasted on your fucking car?"

Despite him asking questions, I knew well he didn't want to hear any actual answers. He just wanted to shout; take his anger out on me because he didn't know what else to do. Mom just stood there, crying. Everything she wanted to say came second to my dad's rage.

"And the fucking nerve you have, stealing my precious antiques--*my* property! Were you trying to sell it? How fucking *dare* you! Those antiques are family history, and you want to pawn them off for some pocket change? Just what do you need that money for, Melbourne? Drugs? Are you on fucking drugs?"

I managed to squeak out a quick no.

"Bullshit," he argued. "What other reason could there possibly be for doing something this stupid? And don't say it's for college! The combination of my money and your student loans are more than enough to buy you food and get your textbooks."

I opened my mouth to speak, but my voice was overpowered by my father's. "What is it you're taking, Melbourne? Crack? Meth? Heroin? What the fuck is so important to you that it involves hurting everything and everyone you know?"

"*Nothing!*" I shouted, desperately trying to take back some level of control. "I'm not taking any goddamn drugs!"

"Stop lying to me!" he screamed.

I threw my hands up. "If you count medication, which was prescribed by a doctor, drugs, then I suppose I'm a fucking pillhead."

My mom finally stepped forward. "You're on medication, Melbourne? What kind?"

"What difference does it make?" I asked, my volume rising with each word. "It's for my health! I take it to stay healthy!"

Dad crossed his arms. "You're *still* lying! There's nothing wrong with you. You don't need medication!"

I growled loudly and turned around. I launched a fist into the wall, causing a hole to form. "You don't know *shit,* you out-of-touch ass-hole!"

Both of my parents rushed over to the damage I had caused. My mother pulled me away and my father gawked at the hole. "Now you're putting *holes* in my fucking house? Give me one reason I shouldn't throw you out right now. Tell me why I should continue paying for your college education!"

I slapped both of my hands into my forehead. "Stop paying for me, then! Kick me out of the fucking house! I'll live on the streets, and hopefully die within a week. Then I won't be your problem anymore. Sadie will be your true pride and joy, and I'll just be a bad memory for the both of you."

At last, Dad seemed to run out of screams. Mom's jaw dropped at my words. I guess I had them scared. On one hand, I wish it didn't have to get to that point. On the other hand, it served them right. It was high time they listened to me.

"Melbourne," Mom said quietly. "Don't say things like that. Please."

"Why shouldn't I?" I probed, tears streaming down my face. "I've been trying to find reasons for *months* now; reasons for *why* I should keep going. If it weren't for the fact that the parking garage at my campus is too short for a fall to successfully kill me, I'd be gone by now. I'd be free from suffering. My inadequate looks and lack of real talent or smarts would wither away into the ether."

Now Dad's jaw dropped. "Are you saying you want to *kill yourself,* son?"

A sob escaped from me. "Unless I can get TerraCure, I'd rather be anywhere but alive. Heaven, Hell, Nirvana, Valhalla, or wherever else may take me. If I'm dead, then at least the visitors will leave. The singing in the walls of my apartment will stop. My inability to form cogent points in class would be no more," at that point, I dropped to my knees, my hands pressing my head down from the back of my head. I choked on my next words, in disbelief that they were coming out in this particular company.

"I-I'd be n-numb to any emotion. No m-more worldly possessions. No more suffering. Just freedom in its purest form."

Both of my parents were speechless. What could they say to that? I supposed they could've had me committed. They could've called an ambulance and had me transported to the ER. They could've even pressured me into going to church, for the purpose of seeking "spiritual healing".

No.

They did none of those things.

Their actual reaction was worse than anything I could've possibly imagined.

"Mel," Dad said quietly. "I have no idea what the hell a *TerraCure* is, but it honestly sounds like some shit sold by some kind of nose-picking huckster. You need *counseling*."

"I agree," Mom said with a nod. "Counseling will do you some good. It will make you feel better. So long as nobody finds out; especially Sadie."

My eyebrows rose. "I wasn't planning on telling anyone, anyway. Why do you think I would?"

They both looked at each other for a moment, eyes telling a story I'd heard many times before. They thought I was being a drama queen. They made the assumption that I was doing this for attention. If I couldn't get praise for my hard work, then I'd lie to get sympathy.

And what do you know?

I was correct.

"We're just...concerned," Mom said, looking back at me. "You've always had a vivid imagination. How do you know this isn't just you thinking too much?"

"It would scare your sister," Dad commented as he too looked back at me. "And everyone else. They'd look at you like you're a freak, and they'd look at us as bad parents."

My brow furrowed.

So, *that* was what it was all about.

Their reputation was at stake.

Nobody wanted to have a crazy kid.

Nobody would *like* a crazy kid.

"I guess I have to lie, then," I decided, turning away from my mother and father. "I have to keep this secret for the sake of the family," I began to walk away. "I'm going to call Maron. Hitch a ride back to school."

"Melbourne, wait," Mom pleaded. "You have to understand where we're coming from."

"I understand completely," I said, refusing to look back at them. "Don't worry. The secret won't leave this house." Mom begged for me to come back, but I was already out the door before she could catch me. I assumed Dad had held her back, instructing her to let me go so I could "clear my head"; whatever that meant.

I stepped off the wooden porch, storming into the driveway. I looked at my father's car and shook my head. How I lamented the loss of my own set of wheels. It was very likely that Dad would refuse to ever help me get another car.

I shouldn't have been in this situation.

I should've been driving off to the antique store.

Nevertheless, there I was.

I guess it was a blessing that none of Dad's antiques were damaged in the crash. He had grabbed a hold of each and every one of them before speeding off. Silverware, fine china, old boots worn by my grandfather, and a couple of empty, glass cola bottles from back when soda first became popular. Even that old grandfather clock that was carefully lodged into my trunk. I was lucky that it was the front end of my car that was destroyed.

Once my feet settled on a spot, I stopped walking and pulled my phone out from my jacket pocket. I quickly scrolled down to Maron's number and clicked. Holding the phone up to my ear, I looked up in the sky. The clouds had darkened, shrouding the sunset. It was going to rain; possibly a storm.

"*Hello?*"

"Hey Maron," I greeted. "I need a huge favor."

She yawned loudly on the other end. I had clearly woken her up from a nap. "*Sure. What do you need, Mel?*"

I looked back at the street. "I kind of, sort of, got in a car accident earlier today. I was hoping you could come pick me up."

All of a sudden, her tone drastically changed from lethargic to highly alert. "*Excuse me, what? What the hell do you mean by "I got in a car accident"? Are you alright?*"

"I'm fine," I lied. "But the car is totaled. I have no way back to campus."

"*What about your parents?*" she asked, tone growing ever more frantic. "*Are they nearby? Are they able to drive you?*"

I sighed. "Look, if you don't want to do it--"

"*I never said that,*" Maron argued. "*Where I was getting at was whether or not they knew about this.*"

"Oh," I muttered sheepishly. "Yeah, they know. But they're really pissed at me. So there's no way in hell they're going to take me back to campus."

I could hear her take a deep breath, likely in the attempt to calm her nerves. "*You'd think they'd just be happy that you're in one piece!*"

I glanced back, eyeballing the trailer. "Yeah, you'd think. But Dad is also pissed because I tried pawning off some of his things."

A brief pause squeezed itself between her and I. "*And why were you trying to do that?*"

"I just wanted to make some money," I stated. "Pay for college stuff. Get the medication that Fairfield gave me. Stuff like that," I looked down at my feet. "So, can you get me or not? If not, that's okay. I'll call an Uber or something."

"*I can get you, Melbourne,*" she said with a hint of frustration in her voice. "*It's just...you were being stupid, dude. There has to be a better way you can make money.*"

I sighed, raising my head back up. "Yeah, I know. I guess I can get a job or something. Like I have much of a choice at this point."

Of course, I knew that was only a half truth.

I still could've sold my Pokemon cards online.

Having sex for money was still an option, too.

"*I'll help you find something,*" Maron assured me. "*Just don't do something like this again, okay? Give me a fucking heart attack.*"

"I'm sorry," I said sincerely. "I'll be more responsible from now on."

Maron sighed. "*Good. I'll be over soon. Where are you, even?*"

"My folks' place. In the front yard."

We said our goodbyes and I ended the call. I squeezed the bridge between my eyes with my fingertips. Maron was right; I *was* being stupid. In my defense, I had a goal I was desperate to meet. She truly didn't understand how urgent it was.

I didn't want to be psychotic.

If I could've chosen to not see fairies in my car, I would've done so in a heartbeat.

Alas, I was pretty much screwed if I couldn't get my hands on that serum.

I shoved the phone back into my jacket pocket. Right on cue, a familiar being flew up to my face out of nowhere. I jumped a little. "*Death*! Don't scare me like that. I've already had a bad day, as it is."

The moth let out a telling squeak.

"It's okay, I assured the insect. "I'm not angry. You just startled me, that's all."

Pleased with my answer, Death flapped its wings and did a little spin. I loved its enthusiasm. The moth was such an excitable creature. How I wished to be that way one day.

"I'm in a really bad way, Death," I said forlornly. "My mental illness seems to be getting worse every day. The medication is taking too long to start taking effect. At this rate, I'll be dead before Aeon Industries makes their money."

Another squeak came out of the moth. This time it was longer, like a cry. I guess it didn't like me saying that. Not that I could blame it for worrying.

"I'm not going to kill myself, friend," I said with clear uncertainty. "I have a mission. I intend on completing that mission."

Death stared at me, silent as a corpse.

"My only regret is that I may never see you again," I commented. "I have a feeling you are not of this world. I can't be sure of much these days, though. For all I know, you're as real as rain."

The moth floated upward, meeting me at eye level.

"For now, let's just enjoy the time we have together," I said with a forced grin. "Of all the otherworldly visitors I've encountered, you're definitely my favorite."

With a satisfied spin, Death finally flew up into the sky. I looked up at it, admiring its beauty. No matter how many times I'd seen the insect, I was always in awe of the coloration of its wings; the skull on its back. Not only was Death aesthetically pleasing, but it had a beautiful personality. Not many people seemed to care about my well-being. I supposed there was Maron, but even she didn't know everything.

And so I watched the moth disappear into the black clouds. Soon after, thunder roared in the distance. Before too long, the sky's tears would pepper the land beneath it.

I hoped Maron would arrive soon.

I didn't need to be caught in the clouds' sadness when I was already contending with my own.

thirteen

Working for the Man

A few days later, I found myself sitting at a table at some local burger joint. I wore a white polo shirt and black dress pants. I figured I didn't need to go in with especially fancy clothing, as working at a fryer likely, and shouldn't, require one to go out of their way to impress bigwigs in suits. I aimed to be a fry cook, not a manager.

I suppose I was lucky that Maron was able to get me a job interview so quickly. Only four days had passed since my car accident. School dragged on, lessons entering one ear and exiting another. My aspirations to become a counselor seemed to be placed on hold. My passion to help others likely wouldn't return until I had the capacity to help myself.

At that point, it appeared that my first step into the world of soulless corporate America would be to flip burgers for minimum wage while the older generations belittled me for not having a *real* job. Oddly enough, that fact did not bother me too much. Of all the things I took to heart, being berated by boomers was not one of them. Who wasn't harassed by old people these days? It appeared that the true initiation into adulthood was to be insulted by an entitled senior citizen who habitually voted red each election. If it happened once, you were an adult. If it happened five-hundred times, it was just another Tuesday.

As I waited for the interviewer to come out to the lobby floor, I twiddled my thumbs as my legs shook. As pathetic as it may sound, that was my first job interview ever. I never bothered too much to find a job while in high school. I was too focused on my grades, as I had high hopes of going to college and making something of myself.

The irony was not lost on me.

I took a deep breath, inhaling through my mouth and exhaling through my nostrils. "Keep it together, Melbourne," I murmured to myself. "It's a part-time fast food job. No need to reinvent the wheel." I tried to focus on my breathing, as I was told to do so while I was receiving treatment at Fairfield.

Focus on breathing.

Focus on sounds.

Focus on smells.

Focus on the sensations hitting my skin.

They called it "mindfulness".

Whilst focusing on my breathing, I eventually shifted to the sounds around me. There were only two customers in the joint. One was a middle-aged man, silenting eating his meal in peace. The other was a young woman, who seemed more focused on typing on her laptop. Her fingertips loudly clacked against the keys on her keyboard, as if she had fake fingernails glued onto her fingers. If I had to guess, she was a fellow student enrolled at my school.

As her typing echoed in my ears, I began to notice the smell of fresh french fries exiting the fryer and being slid into little boxes. The hardness of the seat beneath my ass stood out, cold and uncomfortable. They were all things I was doing to calm my nerves. At the time, it seemed to be working.

Alas, I heard my name called.

The very moment my eyes opened, all feelings of serenity vanished in thin air.

"Melbourne Thompson?"

The voice belonged to a woman, who appeared to be in her early to mid-fifties. She swayed side to side as she walked, her large frame guiding her movements. The woman's hair looked to be light brown, as if she was starting to gray. She wore a green polo and a black skirt with matching tights and closed-toed heels.

Judging by the nametag over her heart, I presumed she was my interviewer. I put on a mask; one that was all smiles and glittering eyes. "Yes ma'am! That's me."

She slowly made her way to my table, clutching a clipboard in her left hand. It was an interesting dynamic presenting itself at that moment. While I was privately panicking over the prospect of having to promote myself to a stranger, she was carefree and glad to take her sweet time in speaking with me. I just wanted her to hurry up. I wanted to get it over with and go back to my apartment.

When six months passed, she finally made it to the table and sat down. "Hello there, Melbourne Thompson. How are you today?"

I chuckled nervously. "Oh, you know. Just reeling from another day of class."

"I imagine," she responded with a grin. "It has to be hard for a handsome young man such as yourself to be bogged down by seemingly daily papers."

I maintained my fake smile, though I was dying inside at her misgendering me. I suppose she couldn't have possibly known, as I looked pretty damn masculine at that moment. Then again, I often chose to present that way due to the closed-mindedness of many strangers. Not to mention that my family shared those beliefs.

"Oh yeah," I forced out. "Thirty to fifty pages once a week is pretty brutal at times. It's not so bad when you copy and paste the abstract for research papers before paraphrasing. But you're still forced to make things up as you go."

She laughed loudly, hurting my ears in the process. "You know, most managers would be turned off by applicants admitting that they take the easy way out in taxing situations."

I bit my bottom lip. *Shit*, I thought to myself. I might've just screwed myself over.

"However," the rotund interviewer continued. "I can sympathize with college students. I remember being in that same boat and doing the same thing. Look how I turned out!"

I nodded slowly. "That's relieving to hear, Miss..." I quickly read her name tag. "...Pamela."

The middle-aged woman cackled. "Please, call me Pam."

"Pam," I acknowledged, letting out another nervous chuckle. "Thank you for understanding, and thank you for giving me the benefit of the doubt."

Pam set her clipboard down onto the table and crossed her arms over it. "So," she began with a tone that contradicted her previous tone of voice. "With that being said, why does an overworked college student want to work at Paul's Burger-Rama?"

Oh fuck, I thought loudly inside my mind.

This was it.

The official beginning of my first job interview.

Could I do it?

Could I land myself a job that would help me fund Aeon Industries in their endeavors?

"Simple, really," I responded with a faux tone of confidence. "I need money for food and textbooks. They don't buy themselves," a third chuckle stemming from an unsettled mind came out of my mouth. "Wouldn't want to flunk my classes because I couldn't read the required texts, you know?"

Pam nodded. "Understandable. You know, I appreciate your honesty. I was worried you'd be another applicant who tried to convince me that you had a passion for fast food," before I could reply, she continued her train of thought. "As long as you aren't honest with the customers, you'll be fine."

I released a fake laugh. "Don't worry, Pam. I know better than to call customers bad names whenever they chew me out for whatever reason."

"What reasons do you believe customers would chew you out?" the manager asked out of nowhere, no doubt the second official question of the interview.

A surge of anxiety sent my heart into a beating frenzy. "*You know.* Any little reason. Maybe their burger was missing its onions. Maybe the cashier was rude to them. Maybe they didn't agree with the prices. Honestly, fast food customers seem to love taking their anger out on employees," I sighed. "I've seen it too many times to count. As a customer, it always hurts my soul when I see somebody berate part-time employees; especially the teenage workers."

She stared at me for a moment, which caused my pre-existing nerves to fray even further. Surely she understood where I was coming from. A woman in her age range ought to be aware of how truly awful fast food customers could be. If she didn't, then I had to question her situational awareness.

Thankfully, a smirk spread across her lips. "You certainly have the mindset of one working in fast food. It's true, we do get a lot of assholes in this joint. It takes a special breed of person to be able to deal with the poor treatment."

I sighed with relief. "Yeah. I believe I'm that person you're looking for."

"Oh really?" she asked. "How have you handled conflict in the past?"

Okay Melbourne, I told myself.

Time to lie your ass off.

"I let it roll off my shoulders. Let people rant and rave. They'll eventually run out of steam and go about their business."

A toothy grin painted itself over Pam's face. "Good answer, Melbourne," she bent down and began writing on the piece of paper clipped onto her clipboard. I dared not to look, as my nosiness could've potentially turned her off from the prospect of hiring me. "I have one last question."

I nodded. "Fire away."

She looked up at me. "When's the soonest you could start?"

A wide smile spread across my face.

Was this it?

Did I land myself the job?

"Immediately," I answered truthfully.

Pam wrote more onto the piece of paper. "Consider yourself hired, good sir! You'll start next week, on Monday. What size do you wear?"

I let out an uncontrollable squeal. "Large, ma'am!"

"Large uniforms it is, then. I'll order those tonight and they should be here before you start. Keep the ringer on your phone turned on. We'll call you whenever they're ready to pick up."

She held her hand out. "Welcome aboard, Melbourne Thompson."

I quickly took her hand and gave it a firm shake. "Glad to be a part of the team, Pam!" My feet tapped against the ground with unbridled excitement. I couldn't believe it; I got the job! Somebody liked me enough to give me a chance!

For once, things seemed to be going my way.

| **fourteen** |

First Day

The uniform was a bit tight around my crotch and the visor looked stupid. Nevertheless, I wore it and didn't verbalize my objections. Pam seemed to appreciate this, as she arrived at seven in the morning, bright-eyed and bushy tailed. She made me think of somebody who was hyped up on five expressos. Or perhaps she had snorted around three or four lines of cocaine.

I felt intimidated by her energy, admittedly.

But I wasn't ever going to let her know that.

"Good morning, team!" Pam exclaimed, all smiles. "Is everyone ready for another glorious day at Paul's Burger-Rama?"

The two female cashiers glared at the manager, disdain etched clearly into their faces. The senior fry cook, who just so happened to be my trainer, gave a quiet thumbs up. Being the fresh meat of the crew, I put on a fake smile. "Yes, Boss!"

Her grin grew larger, showing off her crusty teeth. "I like your enthusiasm, Melbourne. The rest of you could learn a thing or two from our newest member of the team."

The feeling of major awkwardness flushed through me. I slowly turned around and, expectedly, the rest of the team looked at me with disgust. It might've been my choice to be a suck-up at that time, but it didn't mean it was sincere. Being a fry cook wasn't exactly my dream job. Flipping burgers wasn't my passion.

Alas, I wanted to get paid.

And the best way to do that was to kiss ass.

"So," I said aloud as I looked back at Pam. The hateful stares from my co-workers pierced into my skin like freshly sharpened knives. "When do I start my training?"

The large woman pointed at the senior fry cook, whose name tag said *Justin.* "That man over there will show you the ropes. As long as we don't get slammed today, you should have a fairly easy first day."

I turned my head just enough to see the fry cook, who looked to be in his early thirties. He had five o'clock shadow, platinum blonde hair, and bags around his eyes. My assumption was that he secretly hated his job. I couldn't blame him; it's not fun being screamed at by Karens just because you put onions on their burger.

"Come 'ere, kid," Justin ordered, gesturing to me to follow him. I did as I was told, ignoring the hateful glances from the cashiers. Once I was close enough, he entered the kitchen. "Alright," he started off, turning around to face me. "Before we start, do you have any questions?"

Taken aback, I stammered over my words. "Uh-um, well, yeah. I don't know where anything is, where everything is, how it all works, and the protocol with the food."

Justin snorted. "Flipping burgers ain't exactly rocket science. You turn on the grill, place the patties onto the fryer, flip them after a minute, then add the bun and whatever else goes on the customer's order."

I widened my eyes a bit. "Okay, but how do I turn on the fryer? Where do I find the ingredients?"

"You clearly don't cook your own meals," the senior fry cook said with a chuckle. "I've been working in this dump for six years now. I learned all my shit on day one. I expect you to do the same. One explanation should be more than enough for it to stick inside that head of yours."

I swallowed hard.

He was asking for too much.

I wasn't smart enough to learn all of this in one day!

How was I supposed to keep the job?

"I-I'll do my best," I said nervously.

Justin let out another snort. "I don't want your best. I want your *permanent*. Show me how you're going to work for the entirety of your employment at Paul's Burger-Rama."

My eyebrows rose. "I can't show you my, uh...*permanent*...when I don't even know where to find the ingredients for the food. I don't even know the entire menu."

With a sigh, the fry cook held his hand up and gestured to me to follow him once more. "I'll show you the freezer, then I'll show you the cabinets in which the patties and shit are stashed. Satisfied?"

I nodded slowly, humbled by his tone. "Yessir," I answered meekly.

"*Good*," he responded, frustration encompassing his vocal tone. "I assume your mommy didn't pack you a jacket. Sucks to be you, I guess. Because the freezer is fucking cold."

I shrugged behind his back. "I don't mind the cold. It's mainly the hot that bothers me."

"Then you'd be better off working as a cashier," Justin said bluntly. "As the ol' saying goes; if you can't handle the heat, stay out of the kitchen."

I mentally kicked myself. What a stupid thing to say. The man already made it clear that he had no patience for newbie mistakes. I needed to give one-hundred-ten percent if I wanted to keep the job.

"Don't worry about me," I spoke with a faux air of confidence. "I'm willing to sweat a little if it means doing good work.

Justin grunted as he opened a large metal door. As it swung open, I could immediately feel the icy force-field slap my face and torso. I shivered. "You weren't kidding about the cold," I commented cautiously.

"Yeah," he commented nonchalantly. "Don't be surprised if you catch a cold."

Another shiver washed over me like an ocean wave. I hoped the senior fry cook would close the door. Just because I would be forced to step into the freezer at least once a day, that didn't mean I wanted the cold to linger longer than it needed to. "It's, uh, really large," I said awkwardly. "Very spacious. I'm curious about where everything else is, though."

Catching on, Justin closed the freezer door. The relief of lingering warmth from the kitchen settled like eagle eggs in a carefully constructed nest. My skin felt immensely relieved, but it was a temporary peace. Within the following ten minutes, I was thrown to the wolves. I was handed a spatula and insincerely wished the best of luck.

The horde invaded Paul's Burger-Rama within the blink of an eye. It was only me and Justin working the back. He worked the fryer and I worked the grill. It became evident at that point that charm didn't land me the job; desperation did. They were short-staffed and were willing to take any desolate fool willing to work for pennies.

Oh well, I decided.

Sometimes life fed you shit.

And you were forced to eat it with a smile.

"Hey, Fresh Meat," Justin calls out. "We got a number two with no pickles! And a number four with cheese!"

I gulped.

My first order.

A cheeseburger with no pickles, and a chicken sandwich with cheese.

Sounded simple enough, I thought.

Thought being the key word.

With a quick nod, I grabbed a beef patty from out of the small reserve we had and placed it onto the hot grill. Then, I grabbed a chicken patty and placed it a ways away from its sibling meal. My hand clutched the spatula tightly. I watched the food sizzle and crackle. After a minute, I flipped both.

So far, so good.

But, like all things in my life, it didn't last.

"Throw the patty at Justin," came an unfamiliar voice. I looked around as I was grilling. Not surprisingly, there was nobody with me other than the senior fry cook on the fryer. I rolled my eyes and flopped the beef patty onto a bun. I wasn't going to let the voices win again.

I then flipped and scooped the chicken patty onto another bun. After sprinkling the ingredients on top, I served the food. As soon as I was finished, another order came in.

And another.

And another.

Another and, you guessed it, another.

As soon as I thought I had the swing of things, I was then expected to serve up several items at a time. My nerves began to fray. It was only my first day. Why did we have to get slammed on my first day?

"Put your hand on that grill."

The voice came back a little louder that time. That wasn't good, I thought. They were acting up at the worst possible time. I understood that it took a few weeks for my medication to start working. Nevertheless, my life was rapidly falling apart.

"Please," I quietly begged. "Let me have this." At the same time of this plea, I was juggling four number threes, which were double cheeseburgers; one without lettuce and two with tomatoes. My hands were beginning to shake viciously. Alas, the orders kept coming.

"One number four, Fresh Meat!"

"Three number twos!"

"Five number threes, Melbourne! Hurry up!"

I was in a panic. What was a newbie supposed to do in a situation like this? I hadn't even worked a full day! I wasn't some kind of super-hero!

To make things worse, the voice in my head was getting much, much louder.

"*I said fucking put your hand on the goddamn grill! Do it, you coward!*"

The masculine voice, which seemed to have what sounded like a northern accent, was persistent and demanding. He was screaming so loudly that an echo bounced from right to left in my head. The combination of him and the busy shift was starting to do me in.

"Another number three, Melbourne!"

"*I gave you an order, dumbass! Slap that meaty hand onto that grill!*"

"*Please* serve up those patties, Fresh Meat. The customers aren't going to wait all day!"

"*Do it, you fucking pussy!*"

"You forgot the cheese on three burgers, you idiot! Fix them *now*!

"*Melbourne!*"

"Melbourne!"

"*Melbourne!*"

"Melbourne!"

In the tug-of-war between work and psychosis, the psychosis ended up winning. I slapped my free hand onto the grill. My flesh sizzled like the patties I had been serving. I screamed loudly.

"Ah, fucking shit! *Fuck!*"

It pleased the voice, as he finally kept quiet. Unfortunately, the pain traversed from my flesh into my bones. I pulled my hand off the grill and looked at the damage. It was black as day, most likely a first degree burn. My heart practically leaped out of my chest. "Fuck, fuck, *fuck!*"

Justin stomped into the back. "What's the hold up? We have customers! Why can't you–" At that point, he noticed me grasping the wrist of my left hand. One look at my palm and he realized what had happened. "You *moron*! How'd you manage to burn yourself like that?"

I opened my mouth to speak, but no words would come out.

"We don't do worker's comp here! I'm reporting your ass to Pamela! She'll make mincemeat outta you! You might as well consider yourself fired!"

He stomped into the back, toward the manager's office. Tears rolled down my eyes, partially due to the burns and partially due to the anguish. This disorder was truly going to kill me. My life was on a downward spiral.

It was like being stuck in a muddy hole that was too slippery to climb out of.

| fifteen |

Dirty Deeds

"I don't know, Mel," Maron murmured. "You don't even know this guy. What if he's turned off by...you know."

The black skirt complimented the purple crop-top I had picked. The make-up on my face was immaculate, as Maron begrudgingly helped me put it on. Not only was I sure to make money through the endeavor, I also had the opportunity to express my gender comfortably to my heart's content.

Kenny mentioned that he liked them beautiful and strong-jawed.

Guy was certainly a chaser, as my constant dancing on the gender spectrum seemed to entice him.

And I didn't mind in the slightest.

It was all for TerraCure, after all.

"By what?" I asked as I slipped into my black fishnets. "Whatever you're worried about, I've already told him."

The blonde shrugged as she watched me from over my shoulder. "It just seems kind of sudden. You just met this guy online two days ago and you're already going on a date with him."

"I'm an adult, Maron. I'm allowed to have raunchy sex if I so please."

My best friend snorted. "You've never had sex in your life, Melbourne Thompson. You have no idea what you're getting into."

I rolled my eyes as I slid my platform heels out from the box that had been patiently laying on my bed. Being born a male, I unfortunately had large feet. Nothing too unreasonable, but larger than most women. Luckily, the sex shop about ten miles from campus sold the shoes in men's sizes. They came in black, red, and pink. Of course, I chose the black pair; add a little consistency to my planned outfit.

"How hard can sex be?" I asked Maron, naive. "I just suck his dick, right? Then possibly let him take me from behind?"

The blonde laughed loudly. "You have *any* idea how difficult both of those tasks are?"

At this comment, I couldn't help but turn around to face her. She had an amused grin plastered onto her face as she had arms crossed. "I think I know more about the male body than you do, honey," I commented playfully. "I know what men like."

"That's not the issue," Maron elaborated. "First of all, guys rarely ever wash their privates properly. It will taste like old semen, pee, and sweat."

I gasped. "I take offense to that. Not everyone with a penis is that gross."

"Maybe *you* aren't," the blonde said, not backing down from her position. "But most guys are. And the worst part? They never notice, They never take the time to really think about things like that."

I looked away, back at my shoes.

It would've been a lie if I said I didn't feel a little self-conscious at that moment.

"Secondly," Maron continued. "Anal sex really, really hurts. And I have my doubts that this guy will have any lube on him."

I chuckled as I pulled one shoe onto my foot. "Like you've ever had anal sex."

She giggled like a mischievous schoolgirl. "Remember Hank? From Senior Prom?"

I stopped mid-pull. Hank Franklin was a bad boy with a catchy name. He was known to be a bit of a sleaze. He went through girls like he went through cigarettes. He was definitely an eye-catcher, as he was fit and had an attractive amount of stubble to compliment his short sandy hair.

Not surprisingly, he took an interest in Maron.

And she took the bait.

Hook, line, and sinker.

"You didn't."

Maron flashed me a seductive wink.

"You *whore!*" I exclaimed, tossing my shoe box at her. She laughed maniacally as she dodged the object in motion. "You have *no* room to judge me, honey!"

Once her laughter ceased, she shook her head. "I never said I was judging. Just trying to provide my bestie some words of wisdom."

With an annoyed sigh, I turned back around to finish slipping into my platform heels. "If it makes you feel better, I can bring some lotion with me. That should be good enough."

Another cackle left the blonde. "Sure, Mel. Whatever you say."

As I finished slipping into my shoe, I made quick work of the other foot. "But answer me this," I asked with a nervous chuckle. "What if he wants *me* to fuck *him?*"

Maron gave me an exaggerated sigh. "I don't know, Mel. You're on your own there," at that moment, another girly giggle escaped her lips. "But if he decides to go down on you, be sure you've washed up."

"What do you take me for?" I asked loudly. "A *man?*"

At that jab, we both broke into childish laughter. It might've sounded like a silly thought, but I truly feared the day that laughter would no longer erupt from within me. I'd been told before that people on the schizo spectrum eventually got to the point where their emotions felt flat. No happiness or excitement existed in the day of those people; only bitter memories of what was lost.

I refused to let that be me.

Laughter was already hard enough as it was.

Anytime a legitimate laugh came, I cherished it.

I clung onto it.

It helped remind me that I had a soul--a wellbeing.

As I always did, I clung onto what little joy Maron's presence brought me and carried it with me into my date with Kenny...if I could even call it that. We hadn't exactly planned on a romantic evening, candlelight between us as we conversed over a hot meal. It was intended to be more of a dirty tryst, bodies touching as sweat fell off the both of us like tears.

It wasn't for fun, believe me.

Kenny was decently attractive, but he wasn't my type.

White polos, black slacks, fake Jordans, twenty dollar shades that emitted the illusion of being two-hundred dollar glasses, and a naturally brown fade that was dyed bleach blonde; the guy looked like a middle-class douchebag cosplaying a rich man. When we weren't sending sexy texts and pictures to each other, he waxed his ego by talking about all of the nice things he had. He had a slick Camaro, a pool in his backyard, and even a diamond chain he often wore around his neck.

I wanted to be a cheeky asshole about his so-called "wealth". If he was so well-off, why wasn't he treating me to a lovely evening by cruising the city or eating at a fancy restaurant? Why was he taking me straight to a dingy hotel room? Better yet, why was he paying an escort to spend time with him if he was such a big man? His line was cast, but I wasn't taking the bait; more like I was offering a quick nibble before moving on to the next hook.

Alas, I kept my mouth shut.

He was offering me a lot of money.

It was more money than I'd made in a long time, if ever.

I didn't want to screw things up because of my sass.

I waited by the archway of my college campus, leaning against the stone like a bored hooker. The outfit made me feel like a disease addled slut; all I needed was a cigarette and I'd be all set. Not even my bandaged hand would've been enough to discern me as anything other than a lecherous husk. It was either I waited for Kenny to pick me up, or I explained to Maron why we were skipping the formalities and going straight to business. She knew what was bound to happen, but that didn't mean she needed to know the specifics. She didn't need to see the sad state of the two and a half star hotel we were meeting at.

As I awaited this guy's arrival, I looked up into the clouds. Their formation reminded me of smoke rising from a chimney. It even shared the charcoal texture of a fire burning in a cozy home. My prediction involved rain, possibly thunder. I supposed it was too much to ask for a nice, warm cuddle between Kenny and myself as we waited for the storm to pass.

In the meantime, however, a familiar face rushed down from the sky to make my acquaintance once more. In the midst of my dreadful anticipation, I found a reason to smile. "Hello, my friend."

Death, in all of her majestic splendor, fluttered her yellow and black wings in front of me. She showed off her little feet, wiggling them as she hovered over me. As I expected to happen, she squeaked loudly. I smirked. It had come to the point where I wasn't sure if she was distressed, or simply trying to speak to me.

"You here to offer me emotional support?"

Another squeak came from the insect.

"Yeah. I'm not really invested in this...whatever it is. I'd rather be in my bed, curled up in a warm blanket," I sighed, running a hand through my hair. "But I guess it needs to be done. I need a way to make money as I wait for someone to buy my cards online."

She squeaked again.

"Look," I said defensively. "I can't hold down a job. Shit, I wasn't able to even last one lousy day as a fry cook. And I'm not charming enough to make it as a cashier. I'd lose my cool as soon as some aging bitch starts yelling at me."

Death spoke to me again, even louder than before.

"What else can I do? I don't have a car. No job. No family to help me. I can't wait forever for these fucking meds to finally start helping me."

Rather than speaking again, the moth looked at me quizzically-- well, as quizzically as an insect with a tiny face could've. It tilted its body upward, as if watching the darkening clouds.

"You probably need to find shelter soon, little one," I pointed out. "I hear storms aren't too friendly to your kind."

Unable to convince me anymore, Death let out one last defeated squeak before flying off. With a sigh, I watched it flutter off into the ether. I knew I'd see it again soon, with it likely trying once more to communicate a point that I couldn't decipher due to the language barrier between us.

Right on cue, an ocean blue Camaro came rolling up from down the street, stopping in front of me. I sighed. That was for me. I knew I needed to swallow my pride and just get it over with. That didn't mean I was going to enjoy it, however.

The passenger window rolled down, a Caucasian male eyeballing me from over his budget sunglasses. "You need a ride?"

Putting on a fake smile, I winked at him. "You know it. It's going to rain soon. I'd rather not get too wet," I stepped closer to the car. "Well, *prematurely* wet."

Kenny chuckled darkly. "Well then. What are you waiting for? Get in."

Wasting no time, I grabbed onto the door handle and pulled it open. I quickly stepped into the vehicle and was immediately met with the smell of extremely strong cologne. The fragrance should've been enticing, but it just made me feel nauseous. It was as if this man got so carried away with the prospect of getting laid that he just poured the entire bottle of cologne onto his body.

Just breathe, I told myself.

If things went well, then TerraCure would be mine in no time.

As soon as I closed the door beside me, Kenny rolled the window back up. Just before I was able to buckle my seatbelt, he suddenly put his hands on me. His left rubbed the small of my back and his right squeezed my thigh. "I've been waiting for this all day," he murmured as he inched close to my ear.

His hot breath made me shiver. He obviously wasted no time. I'd never met another human being who lusted after me so much that they were unable to control themselves when seeing me. Whether it was for beauty or desperation was a mystery. Either way, it made me feel somewhat desirable.

"Kenny, I--"

The man latched himself onto my neck, his teeth gently scraping my skin as his lips puckered down onto me. He pulled my thigh closer to him, though it wouldn't budge too much due to the console between us. The sensation of his mouth and the urgency of his hands admittedly sent me conflicting feelings. Though, I supposed it was inevitable that such feelings would have come that night, as the nature of shameful sex tended to go down that route.

So I allowed myself to sink into those feelings, closing my eyes and focusing on the sensations he was providing me. It felt like Kenny's tongue slithered out from between his teeth and began dragging in little small circles. A small moan crawled from out of me, which seemed to encourage him. Before I knew it, he let go of my thigh and placed his hand onto my crotch. I had been wearing lacy panties that were large enough to support that anatomy of one such as myself.

He felt how thin they were.

I knew the moment his fingers tightly squeezed the outline of my penis.

Out of shock, I gasped loudly and pushed him away. "Kenny, *please!* Can we maybe hold this off until we get to the hotel?"

I opened my eyes and glanced over at my date. He offered a sleazy, toothy grin. "Sure thing, babe. I wouldn't want anyone else to see you this way, anyway."

And with that, Kenny straightened himself up and shifted the car out of park. We then took off for our honeymoon suite, also known as the Riverside Inn. It was known to be a rather dirty hotel, as most of the reviews online ranged from one to three stars. I seemed to recall a lot of comments regarding unwashed bed sheets and no towels.

I guess I couldn't complain.

I was just going there to bust a nut.

It wasn't like I was moving in.

The drive was an agonizing wait, lasting around fifteen or twenty-ish minutes. During the entirety of the drive, Kenny carried on about his car. It wasn't a hard purchase at all, apparently. He was "effortlessly" about to buy it because he makes "serious bank" as an online rapper. I had a feeling that he was overselling himself just a bit, but I didn't say anything.

In fact, I said nothing during the duration of the ride. Quite frankly, he never asked for my input on anything. He was content with me just humming acknowledging responses to each of his points. An occasional nod and short *oh wow* seemed to suit him well enough.

Once we finally arrived at the Riverside Inn, we parked in a spot right beside a room door, reading "102". Once the car had been shut off, I observed the man unclip his seatbelt and quickly unzip his pants. "We're here, baby. Now for the fun to begin."

I swallowed hard. "You don't want to even check into the room first?"

Before giving me a verbal response, he reached into his beige dress pants. With a swift yank of his underwear, his erection flung out of his fly. I began to feel my heart race, and not in the way Kenny was probably hoping. I wasn't ready for this. I didn't want my first time to be with some sleazy jerk.

Granted, he wasn't a bad size; maybe a little over average. But that wasn't the issue at hand. I lamented the positively shameful acts I had subjected myself to in the name of TerraCure. If anyone had told me a year ago that this was where my life would've been, I would've rolled my eyes and carried on about my day. Alas, there I was.

Was I going to call the escapade off?

No.

Lengths for the venture aside, I still needed TerraCure.

If fucking strange men was what it took to be normal, I would've done it regardless of whatever gripes I had.

"I already checked us into the room," Kenny murmured. "But why don't we do a little foreplay first? Spice things up a little."

I raised an eyebrow. By "foreplay," I had no doubt he meant for me to do something for him while he kept his hands to himself...or on the back of my head. Granted, I didn't want the man touching me. It was bad enough that I was probably going to be on the receiving end of a pounding. That didn't mean I wanted him to touch anything else on me.

"O-Okay," I murmured meekly. "Um, what do you want me to do?"

Kenny waggled his eyebrows. "You're in college. You're a smart one. I think you can figure it out."

I swallowed hard. I knew exactly what he was aiming for me to do, and I wasn't feeling it. I didn't want my mouth on anything attached to this guy's body. The only thing I could feasibly do was play dumb. If he got angry, I could fake naivety

And so, with a shaky hand, I grasped his hardened appendage and began to slowly stroke him. Thankly, this seemed to be an acceptable course of action...for the time being. I knew well he'd eventually grow bored and want me to "spice things up" further. Until then, I sighed with relief and mentally disconnected myself from the acts I was committing.

"Oh yeah," he moaned quietly. "Tighten that grip, baby. I ain't gonna break."

With a quick breath, I did as I was told. He felt moist, as if he were either sweating or somehow got his bits soaked with rainwater. Maron's words echoed in my head. I wasn't going to be surprised if this man had neglected to properly shower before meeting with me.

"*Umph*," he grunted. "Faster, man. *Faster!*"

Wasting no time, I sped up my pace by a hair. His breath came out in quick gasps. So far so good, I thought to myself. And no hallucinations were plaguing me! It appeared the venture might've bore some fruit after all.

And then, the moment I had been dreading came to pass.

"Mmm, baby. That hand feels great and all, but I think there's a part of your body that would feel better around me."

With a defeated sigh, I let go of his penis and looked down at him. I leaned down and wrapped my lips around his genitalia. Sure enough, my initial assumption was correct. Maron was also correct. Much to my misfortune, the guy was not drenched in rainwater.

He was, in fact, sweaty.

Very sweaty.

Like he hadn't bothered to wash his balls during his last shower.

Disgusted, I pulled away and started gagging. Kenny looked over at me with a shit-eating grin. "Too big for you, huh? I've been told that a time or two."

As I nearly got sick in the Camaro, I decided right then and there that this wasn't going to work. As much as I wanted TerraCure, I wasn't physically capable of putting up with this man's hygiene...or lack thereof, rather. And so, without further hesitation, I unbuckled my seatbelt and quickly rushed out of the car.

"Hey!" he called out, dumbstruck by the change of tone. "Where are you going? *Hey*!"

Not looking back, I rushed as quickly away as my heels would allow me. At that point, Kenny began lobbing insults my way. "Slut, "asshole," "bitch," and "cocksucker," were among the most common. I didn't care. I wanted to be back in the safety of my dorm room, looking back on that moment as another miserable day.

I quickly fished my phone out of my skirt pocket and dialed Maron's number.

| sixteen |

A Miracle

Popcorn ceiling looking down on me, I was sprawled out onto the bed in my room. My flatmates were off doing God knows what. Not that I really cared, of course. My life and their lives didn't really mingle all too much. My doings were no skin off their bones, nor theirs mine.

I let out a forlorn sigh. Goddammit, I thought to myself. Dammit, dammit, *dammit*! I was so close. It would've been an easy payday. All I had to do was provide a service to a depraved man. I could've gotten my hands dirty and soldiered through the uncomfortable experience.

But I couldn't even do that. As much as I hated myself, I seemed to still cling onto some level of self-respect. Why, though? There was nothing to respect me for. I hadn't been out of the hospital for the two weeks it took for my medication to start working. Alas, I was still a dysfunctional mess.

How many people my age could say hallucinations ruled their lives? How many could say they wrecked their cars because they were too busy speaking to fairies? What about burning their hand at work because a voice told them to touch a hot grill? I held said hand up to my face, examining the tightly bandaged appendage. Kenny didn't even bother to ask about it, and maybe that was for the best.

With a deep sigh, I laid my hurt hand over my face. Covering my eyes, I felt myself begin to weep. "I'm such a fucking failure," I murmured. "Why can't I do anything right?"

Was this forever?

Was TerraCure a far off dream that would never happen?

Was the prospect of being normal just a laughable, cruel joke?

At that moment, I was thankful nobody else was in the apartment. If they were, they might've been able to read my mind and take me straight back to the hospital. Because, at that very moment, I really wanted to die. I wanted to jump off a building. I wanted my blood and innards spilled over the pavement. I wanted everyone to see the pathetic whelp who couldn't keep going on.

"Nothing's stopping me from doing that," I said aloud to nobody else but myself. "I can take an Uber to the city. Ask to be dropped off in front of an office skyscraper," I smirked at the ceiling. "One of those high-end ones with the parking garage across the street."

I blinked slowly. "With that logic, I suppose I could just jump in traffic," with a quick thought, I shook my head. "Nah, I'm not gonna do that. Every suicidal dumbass in this country does that. Plus, the likelihood of some sociopath hitting me with their car willingly is very low."

I sighed deeply, rather enjoying the company of my own voice for a change.

Nobody inside my head.

Nobody outside my head.

Nobody but me.

"So I guess it's up to my legs and the parking garage ahead of me," I raised my hand up, bending my fingers to mimic a walking motion. "I'll climb up that damn garage, breeze through each floor. If there's an elevator, that's cool, too. But I have my doubts, you know?"

I flattened my hand and raised it even higher.

"Make it all the way to the top. And then..."

I slowly began to drop my hand while making childish "falling" noises.

"*Splat*!" I exclaimed as my palm slapped against my stomach. I then raised my hand a little, curling my fingers to resemble a dying spider. "Just like that. Nothing more than a puddle of meaty chunks."

I snorted with amusement.

"Like beef stew! There we go. I'll be reduced to soup!

I laughed maniacally. I didn't know what was scarier: my morbid imagination, or my genuine laughter over the thought of my own death. Life was supposedly precious, something to be cherished. And yet I laid there, my witch cackle roaring as I imagined my body parts sprawled over the concrete.

I began to accept that TerraCure would never be funded. I knew all was lost at that moment. The only way out was for me to take that final leap. Man's small step met my giant leap.

Understanding what I needed to do, I picked up my phone, which had been lying beside me. Within a few taps, I was confirming my payment for my Uber driver. After submitting, I was informed he'd arrive in fifteen minutes. I took a deep breath and closed my eyes.

For the first time in what seemed to be forever, I felt relaxed. I embraced the calm before the storm. The tension in my neck and shoulders ceased, my back lying completely flat on the bed. A petite smile smeared itself onto my face.

Fifteen minutes.

The drive to the city was a good ten.

It would likely take five to ten minutes to find a parking garage and climb to the top.

So my end was only thirty to thirty-five minutes away; not even an hour.

After a moment, I opened my eyes and stared at my phone screen. The minutes crept. The seconds staggered. My hand trembled as I grasped my cellular device.

Fifteen minutes became ten. I bit my lip. Ten became five. I climbed out of bed and headed outside of my apartment. I stood in the parking lot, awaiting what was supposedly going to be a black Subaru.

I took an excited breath.

Five became none.

I shook with anticipation, but nothing came. I tapped my feet, assuming my driver had gotten stuck in traffic. This was fine, I told myself. He was doing his best.

As the moments drifted, my feet began to tap the ground more quickly. I repeatedly told myself things were going to be okay. They were just caught up somewhere. Surely they were making it their business to get to my location as quickly as possible.

A couple more moments passed and I felt myself begin to lose my patience. "C'mon, dude," I murmured, holding my phone up to check the time. Fifteen minutes had certainly passed; fifteen subtracted and twenty added.

"Where *are* you?" I bit my bottom lip in the poor attempt to control my anger. Another ten minutes passed and I released my teeth's hold. "It shouldn't take thirty minutes to get out here," I growled.

Fifteen more minutes passed and I was pissed off. "Where the fuck is this guy?" I growled loudly, balling up my free hand into a fist. "What am I paying this asshole for? Wasting my time?"

Before long, a familiar squeak sounded in my ears as my little friend zapped from behind me, facing me directly. The insect peered at me curiously, as if asking me a question. I squinted at the moth. I knew exactly what the question was.

"Death," I murmured. "Please let me go. This is the end of the line for me."

It squeaked again, much louder than ever before. It whizzed around my head, stopping before my eyes before letting another squeak boom from out of its body. I blinked rapidly. This creature appeared to actually care about me, but why?

"Listen to me," I begged. "There's no silver lining for me. I can't wait another week or two. This is going to kill me if I don't do something now," I heaved a deep sigh, my consciousness itself trying to process the shitshow playing before my eyes. "Why can't I die on my own terms, then? Better be me that pulls the trigger first, right?"

The moth fluttered up close, wingtips brushing against the bridge of my nose. The creature squeaked again, its cries burying itself into my brain. Two more frantic squeaks erupted from out of the insect.

"Death, please," I continued to plead. "Just let me do this."

With another squeak, the moth zoomed upward and began to flutter to the left. Instead of just leaving me to my fate, Death looked back at me, beckoning me to follow. I stared at first, daring not to leave my spot. With my luck, I'd walk away at the very moment my Uber driver arrived.

Alas, I finally succumbed to the little moth's will and followed as it flew toward the campus library. I looked behind me multiple times during the trek, making sure a black Subaru wasn't arriving an hour later than its expected arrival time. There weren't too many students around, which was a blessing for me. I didn't know if I could stand pretending that I wasn't following a random moth with a skull implanted onto its thorax.

After a few minutes, we reached the library's entrance. Death landed onto the second door of the double-doors. With a quiet sigh, I took the hint and pushed the opposite door open. The bug entered the building and I followed.

Several students took notice as I entered the lobby, but looked away once they realized I wasn't a very interesting sight to behold.

Good, I told myself. No need to bring too much attention to myself. Once Death was finished showing me what I needed to see, I was going to hunt down that Uber driver.

We traversed down a few aisles of books, my eyes scanning the fullness of each shelf as we walked. "Death," I said in a hushed voice. "Where are we going? What's so damned important for me to see?"

One more wraparound and eventually we reached a dead-end. The moth fluttered right and landed on a book that had been partially pulled out from the shelf. "This here?" I asked as I tugged at the book. The insect let go and fluttered upward.

I held the book up to observe the cover.

I squinted up at the fluttering moth.

"Really? A book about you?"

The insect happily spun in a circle as I looked back down. The book was titled *The Stories Told by Death's Head Hawk Moths*. The moth on the cover looked similar to my friend, but was smaller in size and a little pointier. With a defeated shrug, I opened the book and skimmed through the text.

As it turned out, Death was indeed a death's head hawk moth. Unless I was hallucinating the book, it appeared that there were more moths like Death in the world. Even if my friend was a figment of my imagination, at least my madness was grounded in reality. It also appeared that the sexual dimorphism in the species was opposite to that in humans. For us, men tended to be built larger than women; male death's head hawk moths were actually smaller than their female counterparts.

"Ah," I muttered, looking back up at my friend. "So you're a lady moth. Thanks for the clarification, m'lady." I looked back down at the text and turned a few more pages. The vast majority of information I found would've only been relevant if I had decided to adopt Death as a pet. As much as I wanted to, I wasn't totally convinced that she wasn't a hallucination.

Eventually, I came across the section she likely wanted me to see all along. It was a section titled "Cultural Interpretations of the Hawk Moths". After giving her one last glance, I looked back at the walls of text underneath the heading.

Apparently, there are many ways in which the death's head hawk moths are viewed. Some of those ways were more positive, as seeing one could mean that a special metamorphosis was coming. When one shed their skin, they take form as a new being; a rebirth, if you will.

On the negative side, however, seeing a death's head hawk moth could be an omen signalling death. Some anecdotal information was listed within the book regarding a man who lost his wife to breast cancer. This had been back in the 1800s, so he didn't have the luxury of driving her to the doctor for treatment. So he had to resort to treating her at home.

"I used to be a strapping, strong man back in my days working in the lumber yard. Big muscles and an even bigger attitude. Alas, I lost most of that as I aged. Even then, I still carried Agatha up the stairs of our home every single day. Every time I lifted her, she felt lighter and lighter. I knew it was the sickness, but I dared not say anything. My love feared death already; especially when she saw that winged critter with the skull on its back. I saw it once, right before she died. It hovered over her, landing on the tip of Agatha's nose. As the bug let go and flew away, my love was gone."

"So I guess you're good for me, regardless of the narrative," I commented as I looked back up at Lady Death. "Either you'll watch me change, or you'll watch me die. I win either way, it sounds like."

At that moment, my phone buzzed with a text notification. I pulled the device up and saw Maron's name pop up. I typed in my password with my thumb and loaded the message. Once the message took up my entire screen, I read and re-read the message multiple times.

"Remember those dudes who were yammering about Aeon Industries? They're back, and have a some kind of first-come first-serve deal going on. Doubt anyone will come though lol. Bunch of scammers."

My eyes widened.

Those guys were back?

Had TerraCure been funded already?

By what?

Who?

At that moment, a gigantic smile spread across my face. My death-wish turned to dust and the embers in my eyes were re-ignited once more. Life was worth living again, at least for a little while longer. Lady Death was a message for my rebirth, not my death.

Another text message popped up on my phone, this time from an unknown number. I loaded up the message and realized quickly it was from my Uber driver, stating he was fighting off rough traffic.

With a sigh of relief, I began the process of cancelling my reservation.

seventeen

Love at First Sight

As soon as I finished cancelling my Uber trip, I bolted out of the library. Lady Death followed surprisingly well, for such a small creature. I didn't bother to ask Maron where these guys were holed up. Why would I ask? If it were my decision, I'd have my TerraCure without anybody knowing. I dared not embarrass myself more than I already had, considering everything that had led up to that point.

Thus, I managed to traverse across campus loudly while still maintaining some level of discretion; a claim that made no sense to anyone, but was still the case for me. Two dormitories and a football field stood between me and the auditorium. I was no racer, but I sure could gun it like nobody's business. Nothing was going to stop me from fixing what previously seemed unfixable.

I had my doubts that there would be a lot of people waiting to try TerraCure. Nobody seemed too thrilled with the offer Aeon industries was trying to sell. I viewed this as an advantage for me. Truly, this meant I'd be first in line.

But what about money, I thought to myself as I passed the two dormitories. Wouldn't I need to pay them for their services? Surely I could work something out with them. Surely I could touch their hearts with my plights. Perhaps I was pathetic enough to warrant a free treatment of TerraCure.

But what if I couldn't?

What if they turned me away?

No, I decided.

I wasn't going to let them tell me no.

If anyone needed this serum, it was me.

Adrenaline soaking through every pore of my flesh, I sprinted around the football field, careful to avoid any sweaty athletes who might've been crossing my path. I looked behind me and, somehow, Lady Death was still keeping up with me. She must've wanted me to see this through. She saved my life, after all. Why would she go through all of the hassle just to watch me die anyway?

Past the football field and I was only a couple feet from the auditorium. To my surprise, a couple of students were waltzing into the facility. Were they there for Aeon Industries, too? Or was something else transpiring in that building?

I held my arms out as I ran, ready to push the door open upon my speedy arrival. I'm sure I looked like a cartoon character at that moment, running frantically toward the cheese on the hook, the hanging sandwich with nothing but my name in it. Alas, my attempts to speed up the trek faltered as I found myself being knocked back. My arms had hit the door the same time as a group of students came walking out. Four outnumbered one and I fell onto the ground.

Trying to ignore the *ows* and *oohs*, I tried to get back onto my feet without acknowledging the voices.

"Hey, you okay?"

"Watch where you're going!"

"Could've gotten someone hurt!"

"Fucking *loser*!"

Once I was up, I pushed past the gawking crowd and headed inside. "Made it," I huffed as two girls walked past me, giving me awkward looks. As I looked up, I was surprised to see a line going up to the stage, where the two representatives from Aeon Industries sat at a single table.

So much for being "the first human test subject".

I whistled. "Damn. I guess more people wanted TerraCure than I thought." Without any further hesitation, I jogged up to the back of the line. I accidentally bumped into the guy ahead of me, who turned around and smiled. I clammed up when I realized it was the hunk from Dr. Barris's class.

"S-Sorry," I squeaked. "I didn't mean to bump into you, Gabriel."

The guy tilted his head a little. "C'mon, man. We've been in class together for long enough now that you should know my name."

I instantly blushed. *Fuck*, I thought to myself. I referred to him by the pet name my mind had formulated for him. Dammit! "Sorry about that, Tom."

He chuckled. "They were go, Melbourne."

I returned his chuckle, rubbing the back of my head. "So, uh, TerraCure, huh?"

"Yeah," he sighed. "I thought I'd be the only one here, honestly. But I guess I should've known better. It's a serum that can erase any bad qualities one has, after all. Who wouldn't want that?"

I smirked. "I suppose you're right. Everyone has a shameful trait they wish were gone. Something they'll take to their grave."

Tom let out another sigh. "Ain't that the truth."

Before I could respond, two more familiar faces emerged from my peripheral vision. Walking away from the stage were my two other friends, Kimberly and Johnny. I whistled at them. "Ay guys!"

Johnny's head whipped around in my direction. "Ay, Mel!"

Kimberly then looked at me and smiled awkwardly. "H-Hey. Fancy seeing you here," she pulled Johnny by the hand and stepped closer to me. "We really weren't expecting to see you or Maron here."

"Well, *you know*," I said in a hushed voice. "Who wouldn't want to get a piece of this serum? Can fix so many things about people."

"We really aren't here for that," Johnny intervened, dare I say defensively? "Me and Kim are just volunteering. Helping these kooks by kicking troublemakers out."

"That's right," Kimberly said with a nod. "Lots of assholes come in here to mock their serum, so we kindly escort them out of the auditorium. Easy pocket change for us."

I clenched my teeth, kicking myself for another unnecessary embarrassment. "Ah, I see."

Johnny looked over his shoulder. "So, uh, what about you? What brings you here?"

My throat closed up, as if regurgitating a fat toad. "Um, well, I- I'm like you. Yeah, I'm working security," I patted Tom's shoulder. "Us both. We're working security, too."

Tom cleared his throat. "Y-Yep. That's us. Two security workers, just guarding the back of the line."

Kimberly nods slowly. "Smart. Making yourselves look like customers to throw people off, right?"

"That's right," Tom blurts out. "Nobody would expect it. We guard the back of the line while you guard the front, right?"

"Well," Kimberly said. "We were actually leav--"

"That's *precisely* what we're doing," Johnny said, interrupting his girlfriend. "We were just checking out the back of the line before help came in. It looks like you guys finally made it."

"Y-Yes," Kimberly stammered. "It took you guys long enough."

We both rubbed the backs of our heads. "Well, you know how things go," I mumbled, stepping ahead once the line moved a smidge. "Being stressed college students tends to make us less situationally aware at times."

The couple looked at each other and nodded. "Right," Johnny commented with a quick breath. "So, we should probably go. Ian and Phil wanted us to go grab some lunch for them."

"And it takes both of you to do this?" Tom asked slyly. "That usually only takes one person, unless it's a lot of food."

"Oh, it's *definitely* a lot of food," Kimberly said a little too quickly. "Those two have the combined appetite of a dinosaur. In fact, we need to go right now so they don't have to wait too much longer," she tugged Johnny's arm again. "Like, *right now.*"

The couple then hurried off toward the auditorium's exit. Within a few seconds, they were gone. Tom and I sighed and looked at each other. "Thanks man," he murmured. "I don't think I could've handled telling them I was here for that serum."

"Honestly, me neither," I admitted. "Some things need to remain secret."

For a moment, we quietly look at each other, exchanging smiles. As beautiful as he was from behind, he was an even better sight to behold up close. Those dark brown eyes of his glowed under the auditorium light. and his pearly whites accentuated his cute face.

If I didn't fancy him before, I certainly did then.

And I was positive he fancied me, too.

The line eventually shrunk some more, allowing us to step closer to the two divine redeemers seated upon their cold metal thrones. Before too long, I would be on the direct highway to normalcy. The nightmare known as schizoaffective disorder would finally end, placed into a box and locked up within the darkest shelf within my memory.

Twelve people soon became nine.

Nine then became six.

And six became four, only two people ahead of us.

Tom and I stood in anxious silence during the duration of our time in line, occasionally making small-talk about the line and people who left after their consultation was over. The minutes ticked and tocked. I wasn't sure if those people were simply humoring the two scientists or actually scheduling appointments. All I knew was that my heart threatened to burst out of my chest the closer we got.

Before too long, Tom was called to speak with the representatives of Aeon Industries. "Nice talking to you, Melbourne," he commented. "We should hang more often."

I smiled, a faint blush likely spreading across my face. "We should. Take care."

As he walked up onto the stage, I watched with curiosity and anticipation. I wondered what was so horrible that Tom felt the need to seek out the services of Aeon Industries. What was his dirty little secret? Was he mentally ill like me? How ironic that would've been, in the grand scheme of things?

It wasn't important, I decided.

He didn't pry into my business, so I shouldn't pry into his.

Tom spoke with Ian and Phil for around ten minutes, give or take. I assumed they had a questionnaire for him or something of a similar nature. He was hunched over the table, but he faced the two scientists rather than the hard surface beneath him. So they didn't have him writing anything, I noted. It appeared I'd only be speaking with them.

Once Tom finally walked off the stage, Phil eyeballed me and motioned for me to come forward. I hurried up to that table. "Hey," I squawked, my feet loudly clopping against the floor in front of the two scientists. "You have no idea how much I've been wanting this opportunity, guys."

The two men looked at each other, the blonde pushing his glasses up. "That's great to hear," he looked back at me with a soullessly professional grin. "You're the guy who wanted help with your schizophrenia, right?"

My eyes widened. "You remember me?"

"Of course we do," Ian chimed in, pushing up his own pair of glasses. "You're the only one who has reported that particular condition to us. We've heard bipolar disorder, depression, anxiety, and even a few unsavory fetishes. Never schizophrenia, aside from you."

I awkwardly rubbed the back of my head. "It's, uh, actually schizoaffective disorder."

The two men shrugged. "Potato, po-tato, dude," Phil remarked. "Two sides of the same coin."

I chuckled nervously. It's okay, I told myself. They were the experts. They knew what they were talking about. I was the uninformed customer, after all.

Yeah," I said, clearing my throat. "I guess you're right. Either way, I'm, uh, here to fix that."

"I imagine so," Phil said with a quick nod. "Luckily, we can help with that."

Ian reached under the table and pulled out a wooden clipboard. "If you may. Go ahead and sign your John Hancock on this list. There's only one spot left, so you chose the perfect moment to come speak with us."

I felt my breath stop in my throat. "TerraCure is taking off that fast?"

"Is it really any surprise?" Ian asked. "A chance to rid oneself of all self-loathing is one sexy deal. Call it the apple in the Garden of Eden, and we're all Eve."

I smirked, taking the blue pen from out of the clipboard's metal clamp. "I'm curious," I commented as I proceeded to sign my name on the last little line of the form. "How did you guys manage to raise money so quickly? It seemed like you guys were essentially booed off the stage during the last visit."

Phil cleared his throat. "Don't worry about that. We have our own solutions to these kinds of problems."

"In with the right crowd?" I asked as I jotted down my phone number.

"You can certainly say that," Ian remarked with a chuckle. "But jumping back to the main point here, we're expecting to have our lab set up within the next few days. We'll call you and go from there."

As I finished writing down my email address, I set the pen down. It was done. I was signed up to receive TerraCure. All would grand in due time.

"Thank you guys so much. I truly mean it from the bottom of my heart."

Phil nodded. "Anytime. Take care."

With a chipper nod, I walked toward the end of the stage as they announced the end of sign-ups to the rest of the people in line. I was on Cloud 9. My troubles were to be extinguished soon. No more psychosis for Melbourne Thompson.

It was over.

I could breathe again.

| **eighteen** |

The Fateful Onboarding

Three agonizing days passed before I heard anything back from Aeon Industries. I made it a point to fly under the radar. Having one class a semester had its benefits; I only had to email one professor whenever I needed time off from class. My line of logic was that I could deliver little white lies to those I knew. I told him I was sick and would be out for a few days, and he ate up my lies like candy.

I figured Aeon Industries would cover for me.

If not, then I'd be able to bounce back.

TerraCure would make damn sure of that.

Maron nearly exposed me as a fraud one day. She had been worried about me, since I wasn't around for a while. "*You're sick?*" she asked. "*Want me to come over and keep you company?*"

I once again conjured up lies. I told her I was highly contagious and she accepted my word as gospel. I'd be lying if I said I didn't feel bad about pushing her away like that. She'd always been there for me, after all. Why would she not be there for me that time?

Because she was biased.

If I had told her about my mental illness, she would've tried talking me out of TerraCure.

I appreciated her opinion; I really did.

But I wasn't going to let her influence me.

Not this time.

The phone call came roughly around six-thirty in the evening. I had just finished taking a shower, albeit a quick one to avoid any pesky hallucinations that might've wanted to emerge before me, visually or otherwise. I would've taken much longer, as I hated feeling grimy. But with as aggressive as my psychotic symptoms were, I didn't want to take any chances.

So I took off my clothes.

Turned on the hot water.

Stepped in and bathed for five minutes.

Then emerged from the shower, skin boiling and clean.

A few minutes later, Aeon Industries called me. I didn't recognize the number and I nearly acted on instinct and denied the call, just in case it was a spam call. However, a strong feeling overwhelmed me, telling me to take a chance and answer.

"*Hello,*" said what sounded like a girl around my age. "*Is this Melbourne Thompson?*"

I answered the lady within milliseconds of a heartbeat. She stammered at my hasty tone, but was able to maintain professionalism. I had to give her props; I probably would've struggled with the act of soldiering onward after being robbed of the full four seconds it took to draw a line between mind and mouth.

"*R-Right, yes. Hello, Melbourne,*" she cleared her throat. "*My name is Rachel. I'm calling on behalf of Aeon Industries.*"

I bit my lower lip in anticipation. "Y-Yeah, hey. I signed up for TerraCure a few days ago."

"*Correct,*" she commented cheerfully. "*Are you still interested in our services, Melbourne?*"

I bit harder into my lip, forcing back an excited squeal. "Yes, ma'am! I am *very* much interested in TerraCure. There's really nothing I'm looking more forward to."

She let out a soft giggle. "*That's great to hear. I'm actually calling to set-up your procedure.*"

I let go of my lip. "Procedure? I thought TerraCure was a pill or injection type of thing."

"*Not quite,*" Rachel explained. "*We have to get your blood acclimated to the serum before you can enter the maintenance phase of your treatment.*"

I nodded slowly. "So, it's like an infusion?"

She cleared her throat. "*I can't really say for sure. I'm just a secretary. You'll have to ask Ian and Filmore about it.*"

"I understand," I said with a chuckle. "When's the soonest you can have me in?"

The sound of fingers clacking against a keyboard tickled my ear. "*Well, you may need some time to prepare for the procedure. Give the heads up to your teacher and all that good stuff. Let your friends know you may be busy for a while.*"

I breathed calmly through my nose. I assumed she meant that I cover my ass and ask for time off from any prior engagements I had planned. I had heard that IV treatment could be an all-day affair; whether it be ketamine, chemotherapy, or some other kind of special blood infusion.

"Can I come in now?"

Rachel was silent for a moment, slowly creeping into another stammering fit before properly answering my question. "*Uh, um, well, I-uh, are you sure, Melbourne? This procedure will take a while. It's really recommended that you give everyone some kind of notice first.*"

I smirked. "They'll be fine. I assume you guys are going to write me up a doctor's note, right?"

"*Y-Yes,*" she answered. "*We can certainly do that. Are you sure you want to do this right now? This is a big procedure. It can, and will, take up a lot of your time.*"

I shrugged as I ran a hand through my damp head of hair. "Listen to me, Rachel. I need this. I need this very badly. The sooner I have TerraCure in my system, the sooner my quality of life will improve for me to not want to kill myself."

Another moment of silence squeezed itself in-between my end of the call and hers. What I had said no doubt startled her a little. If I were her, I would've hung up right on the spot. Alas, Rachel once again impressed me by going the friendlier route of trying to professionally end the call as quickly as she could.

"That's, um, great to hear. Yeah, that's great to hear, Melbourne. Come by the science building in the next hour and they'll get you squared away."

I agreed to her terms and ended the call right then and there. I slipped my feet into my sandals and booked it for the science building, which wasn't too far away from my apartment. Regardless of how long the procedure was going to be, I hadn't the slightest care about anyone else at that moment. All that mattered was getting TerraCure into my system before I got myself, or someone else, severely hurt or worse.

What would've normally been a five minute walk had been reduced to a two minute sprint. Once I reached the front entrance, I stopped long enough to catch my breath. "I wonder if I'll have better lungs after this," I wondered aloud.

This was it.

My delightful little reckoning.

With a deep breath and shaky hands, I opened the door to the science building. The lobby was empty with a hallway split between two walls in the middle. Many posters advertising upcoming school events plastered every free spot on the periwinkle walls. A staircase sat horizontal, heading up to the right side of the building.

At face value, the building was barely worth standing.

However, the presence of classrooms and two large labs justified the continued lifespan of the dusty old facility.

I looked at the pinboard to my left, scanning the sign for directions. Once I found the words "Aeon Industries" casually tacked letter by letter, I noted they were on the first floor, which was the spare laboratory across the geology classroom. I headed in that direction, my footsteps echoing in the empty lobby.

Once I arrived at the door, the first thing I noticed was the audible sound of something bubbling loudly enough to be heard over what was likely a machine motor's fan. I realized knocking would've been a fruitless action to take. So I wiped the sweat coating my right hand off by rubbing it against the bottom of my shirt. Without further ado, I opened the door to Aeon Industries.

It was something out of a sci-fi movie. The room was dimly lit, one side holding a very large table with vials, flasks, and scattered notes surrounding two chemistry sets resting beside one another. Within the glass sets, glowing fluids of tangerine orange bubbled and flowed through the clear funnels and pots. Adjacent to the table were several humming machines, possibly generators of some kind.

Next to those machines laid large glass test tube tanks. There were many of them along the lab, and all of them had the same orange fluids as the chemistry sets. The oddest part of the lab certainly weren't the tubes, or at least not entirely. It was the people that were the most jarring for me to see.

I thought maybe they were mannequins, used as decorative pieces as a means to provide amusement for the scientists. Bodies each floated within the tanks, masks over their noses and mouths. Their arms and legs had black cuffs wrapped their meatiest ends. Each of them were as naked as newborn babies.

I inched closer to the first tank, which housed a beautiful girl of Asian ancestry. I looked up and down at her, admiring the piece of art Phil and Ian had put up in their lab. Once I moved closer to examine the straps around her thighs, I made the startling observation that her skin actually looked to be squeezed. It wasn't a ceramic model, not if that flesh had anything to say about it.

I swallowed hard.

"People," I murmured to myself. "*Real* people!"

As I further observed each bright orange tank, I saw a few familiar faces. I hadn't known many of their names, but I recalled passing them by several times on campus; a few casual *hellos*, nods of acknowledgement, superficial smiles, or even nothing at all. The looks never shied away from tacking little fears into my brain, lungs, and heart. Words, which were undoubtedly spoken telepathically, echoed in my head.

Freak.

Loser.

Failure.

As much as I wanted to scream every time, I knew I'd only make things worse for myself. But at that moment, I no longer needed to scream. I no longer heard their voices. Their eyes were no longer locked onto me.

It was my turn.

Yes, it was my turn to stare, to judge, even.

As I walked down the aisle of test tube students, I looked at each and every one of the naked bodies submerged within the orange fluid. I eventually ventured forth into exceptionally familiar territory. In two neighbor tanks, Kimberly and Johnny shared space with what I gathered was TerraCure.

I smirked. Even in incubation, they were inseparable. If they had the opportunity, they likely would've shared a tank together. It was surely a tragedy for the two of them, as it was uncertain when they'd be released.

Would they feel the same way about each other? What would've changed? If my assumption about the fluids were true, then that meant big changes were coming their way soon. Either way, I saw more of those two than I ever wanted to.

A few more bodies down and I found Tom. Unlike Johnny and Kimberly, who had lied about their agreed upon interest in TerraCure, I didn't find as much amusement in seeing him. Granted, I hadn't the slightest idea what he could've possibly wanted to change. His body was finely tuned and handsome, with and without clothing.

Maybe he was like me, after all.

Changes needed to be made inside, not out.

"Tom," I murmured. As I backed up and turned around, I was instantly startled by Ian standing mere inches from me. "*H-Hi there,*" I gasped loudly.

"Good evening, Melbourne," he greeted with a smile. "Rachel told us to expect you. Said you're pretty hyped for TerraCure."

I cleared my throat awkwardly and rubbed the back of my head. "Y-Yessir. That's me. Hyped up and ready to go. That's certainly me."

The poindexter smirked. "So I see. Luckily, we already have a tank fully prepared for you."

I coughed, looking back and forth between him and the row of tanks. "I-I kind of figured that was why these guys were all here. I guess I just have some questions before we start."

"Ask away," Ian said, crossing his arms. "If you're going to be a participant in our experiment, you deserve to know what you're getting yourself into."

I straightened up my posture. Okay, I told myself. I needed to not be so damn excited for this serum, lest I scare him into denying me the very thing that would've fixed all of my problems. But I also didn't want to be too hesitant, lest he tell me to leave because I "wasn't ready" for TerraCure.

Happy medium, I repeated to myself like a mantra.

Happy, happy medium.

"How is the serum administered?" I asked with a faux air of confidence. "How long will I be in that tank?"

Ian smiled and gestured toward Tom's tank. "So those cuffs? There's an IV within each of them. At all moments of the duration of his hibernation, he's being pumped full of TerraCure."

"Why so many?" I asked. "Isn't one IV enough?"

"Yes and no," the poindexter answered with a half-nod. "While it's true that regular IV fluids spread into the bloodstream, it's simply not enough. We're terraforming the genetics of each and every one of our patients," he casually placed his hand onto my shoulder. "You, Melbourne, are going to be hooked up tightly for the next week. Once you're done, you'll be a new man."

My eyes widened. "A *week?* It's going to take that long?"

"Indeed," Ian said. "Your absence from class will be taken care of. The Dean has personally approved of this project. He will ensure that you aren't penalized for missing a week's worth of class."

I stood there, speechless. I looked back and forth between the tanks and Ian. Was this really happening? Was I really willing to sacrifice a week's worth of knowledge for the sake of becoming the perfect version of myself?

Yes.

Yes, I was.

"I'm game," I said confidently. "Where do we begin?"

Ian slid his hand down to my bicep and nodded toward the end of the aisle of tanks. "Right this way. Let's unearth the real you."

And so we walked to my tank.

The rest was history.

| nineteen |

The Mind of the Embyro

I don't know how long I floated within that tank before my heart began to beat harder than the drum solo of a hardcore metal song. Was it minutes, hours, or even days? Ian had mixed sedation medication into my batch of TerraCure. It was said to be strong enough to knock out a bull. "You'll sleep very well for the next week," he told me as I was hung within the tank, held up by clear wires.

The initial awkwardness of Ian seeing me naked dissipated as the black cuffs were wrapped around my thighs. Their hidden needles shoved themselves into my flesh once they were secure. I yowled in surprise as I felt the sudden pinch. "*Geez*," I gasped. "You don't give us any warning, do you?"

Ian didn't respond, as he was more focused on strapping my upper half up in cuffs. Once they, too, were secured over my biceps, Ian lulled me to sleep with a smile and mantra. "Your birthday is coming."

And so I rested in my chamber, my brain bouncing around the inside of my head like wet clothes in a washing machine. Everything ached. Everything pulsated, pumping fast and faster without any combustible relief. My entire body was in pure agony, and I couldn't do anything but float within the warm abode that was TerraCure.

Ian's voice echoed in my head.

"Your birthday is coming."

"Your birthday is coming."

"Your birthday is coming."

My breathing proceeded to operate within functional capacity inside my mask. My lungs ached as if I were constantly coughing up smoke, but they otherwise seemed content with acting as though my body was experiencing a poor night's sleep. All of my organs felt the pain pierce through their tissue. But everything that needed to function was still functioning, and everything that needed to be halted was halted, such as my stomach and bladder.

Being a science experiment felt wrong.

But Ian's words continued to repeat in gentle whispers.

"Your birthday is coming."

The wildest part of the experience was definitely the visions within my mind. My limbs were destined to act as pin cushions while my thoughts rested in a cozy chair as TerraCure gently dabbed their faces with blush. I supposed that my initial complaint was Ian and Phil's primary focus. I guessed fixing my broken brain required agonizing servitude from the rest of my body.

I looked at it as if one were blind. Their eyesight might've been gone, but their hearing couldn't have been better. Alternatively, one could look at the difference between a smart man and a stupid man. The smart man had brains, but no brawn; vice versa the other way around. I was legally crazy, so my physical adequacy needed to suffer in order for my craziness to disappear.

In the meantime, I was preparing myself for the long goodbye with the part of my brain I wished had never manifested. For a solid week, I was in a turbulent relationship with my thoughts. I'd sometimes see beautiful visions of hopes, dreams, and fond memories I thought I had forgotten ages ago. But on the other hand, I'd see not-so-pleasant images and film reels. I will say, however, that the negatives felt like they were actively being escorted out of my brain like a scorned lover.

They got their last screams in. The visions made it clear that they were willing to put up a fight against the impenetrable force that was TerraCure. Times I was mortified, times I was depressed, the dark side of my mind tried hard to get a few more slaps in before being exiled forever.

They fought.

Yes, they fought.

If it weren't for TerraCure, they would've won.

My favorite vision, by far, was one in which I was standing in a field of sunflowers. The sun shone brighter than a cluster of fire pits burning, and the grass was fresh and green. The temperature was just right; not scorching and not freezing. A light breeze washed over my face while the warmth from the sun covered my bare body like a weighted blanket. The grass blades nestled between my toes as the bottoms of my feet rested firmly on the ground.

I was naked and content; naked and fearless. There wasn't a single sign of danger in the vicinity. I occasionally saw glimpses of butterflies fluttering about, but I'm convinced they were nothing more than flashes of light gifted by the Sun. I was alone. Not even Lady Death appeared within my dream. Honestly, I wouldn't have minded a few woodland creatures to join me, but I was okay to settle for solitude. After all, it was said many times before that the most efficient way to nirvana was through self-reflection and acceptance of the cards we're dealt.

Of course, I supposed there was a lesson to be learned in this. If all it took to reach spiritual satisfaction was to accept myself for the way I was, I never would've needed TerraCure at all. But that's just not how things work. How could I accept myself for all the hallucinations I'd been dealing with? It didn't matter that my medication was in the process of fixing my problems; the fact I needed medication at all was already a major problem.

I didn't want to take the pills.

I didn't want to wait things out.

I wanted to be free and clean.

I wanted to be normal.

TerraCure was my only shot at that.

The sunflower field vision was the longest dream I'd ever had. I guessed that the serum had figured out where my happy place was and locked me in while it worked its magic. It was a little lonely at times, but the silence was well worth it. No voices, no unsavory characters dancing before me. It was me and me alone, and I couldn't have been more joyful. If I'd been awake, I might've even cried.

I'm not sure how long I was there. Minutes? Hours? Days? Ian had told me that I'd be a test tube specimen for a week tops. But time was merely a concept whenever one is stuck within the Hollywood picture show that was their brain. What was short might've lasted ages, and what was long might've been as long as a sneeze. Any bad memory was kicked out in favor of me returning to that field.

But I think my brain gathered when it was time to return home, for the field eventually began to disappear. The sunflowers vanished into pixie dust, the grass blew away into gusts of wind, and the sun blinked just before disappearing as well. I wanted to be sad, I really did. But I think I was ready to wake up. I'd been alone long enough, and I had plenty of time to reflect.

My blinks grew heavier with each flutter. The warm air gradually turned to cool muck. My breathing soon felt confined to the small cave formed by my mask. And with one last blink, I was alive again.

Phil and Ian were on the other side of the glass.

They smiled at me.

"Happy birthday, Melbourne Thompson."

| twenty |

Angel Daze

The remaining serum gurgled as it seeped down into the drain. My body felt like it had just been thawed from a block of ice. I shivered so hard I nearly started convulsing onto the wet floor. Ian and Phil looked down at me, observing but not intervening.

"You'll adjust to the temperature soon," Phil informed me. "Just give it a little time."

I gasped loudly, desperately hugging myself for what little warmth I could muster. "F-Fuck," I yelped. "Jesus *fuck*!"

I moaned and groaned for a little over a minute as the two scientists looked down at me, my naked body writhing. Before long, the room gradually grew warmer, as if somebody was manually adjusting the room's temperature. For all I knew, Phil and Ian were the only scientists employed within Aeon Industries. There was that girl who called me, Rachel. Did she turn the AC down as those two clowns watched me suffer? Or was my body doing just as they said it would?

I let out a few more huffs before the goosebumps all over my body began to recede. "Jesus," I breathed. "You show absolutely no mercy to your subjects, do you?"

"That would defeat the purpose of TerraCure," Ian explained.

"Yes," Phil chimed in. "It's working on its own to fix your imperfections. If we intervene now, it might coax the serum into relaxing a little too much. We can't have that, and neither can you."

Once the chilled numbness in my hands dissipated, I pushed myself up onto my ass. I hugged myself once more, looking all around me. Nobody else was left within the neighboring tanks. It appeared I was the last of the subjects to be released.

"How do you feel?" Phil asked. "Cognitively, I mean. Any dizziness? Brain fog? Disorientation?"

I shook my head. "N-No. Aside from the cold, I feel okay," at the realization of what I had said, I began to glow. "I feel okay, maybe even fine."

The two scientists looked at each other. "What do you mean by that?" Ian asked.

My eyes widened as I quickly got up onto my feet. "I don't feel depressed," I began moving my arms animatedly, talking with them almost. "I'm not depressed! I-I want to explore. I want to learn. I want to love. I don't even feel embarrassed right now! You both are looking at me while my junk is hanging out in the open and I'm fine. I couldn't be happier!"

Phil pursed his lips. "Right. We need to make sure this is actual progress, and not just mania leftover from your mental illness."

My teeth chattered. "Why does every happy feeling have to be mania, though? I feel great. I don't want this feeling taken away from me. This is the first time I've felt truly happy in a long time," I began pacing around the two scientists. "I feel open, okay? I feel free. If I don't hallucinate anytime soon, then I just may scream the praises of TerraCure into the clouds and stars!"

Phil began to open his mouth, but was stopped by Ian placing a hand on his shoulder. "It's too early to tell if this is mania, Phil. Let's give it some time. Melbourne can come see us again in a week or two and we'll see what's really going on."

I looked back and forth between the two men, waiting to hear my next step. Butterflies flapped their wings all the way up to my throat. I was excited. Was that truly the first day of the rest of my life? Was the world my oyster from that point on?

"Well, Melbourne," Phil said with a soft smile. "It looks like things are settled. We'll have Rachel call you in two weeks. If you have any concerns that arise during that time, give us a ring."

I smiled wide, nodding my head hard. "Thank you so much. You guys might've possibly saved my life." I meant those words more than I meant for my gender identity to be taken seriously. My eyesight seemed brighter, sharper. Pictures were more crisp, as if that was what they were meant to look like. My shoulders felt light, as if all my burdens were whisked away. Even my heartbeat was easy, despite my excitement.

Did I have problems outside of that moment?

Certainly; my parents were still angry with me, I lacked a car, I had disappeared for a week, and I was way behind on my schoolwork.

But those seemed like minor inconveniences at that point.

"I could honestly cry right now, I'm so happy," I said loudly.

The two men both gave me small grins. "Well, no need to cry," Ian commented. "This is now a smooth journey going forward."

"Shit," Phil chimed in. "You might even find yourself bored before too long when you notice nothing really phases you anymore."

I cackled. "Boring is fine by me! Better than seeing weird people and things every day. Better than making a fool of myself for no reason!"

"That's a fair point," Ian stated. "In that case then, let's get your clothes. We took the liberty of washing them while you were asleep."

"And you can worry about the bill next time we speak," Phil said. "Be prepared, though. It will be a rather steep one."

Another laugh escaped from my mouth. "I'm sure I'll get it handled!"

As Ian wandered off, I stood there shaking. My troubles were over. I'd risen above the challenge and was now reaping the rewards. There was no longer a reason to fret or cry.

I'd won.

| twenty one |

Walk With Me

The first full day of TerraCure felt like a dream laced with freshly invoked contentment; contentment often found when high off of a ripe batch of cannabis. The haze spun around my head, but I felt fully oriented. The world was on fire behind me, if everyone's reactions to me returning from the dead were anything to go off of. Maron yelled at me, as did my parents when I finally returned their missed eight or nine calls. Dr. Barris threatened to flunk me until I provided the doctor's note given to me by Rachel.

People were worried.

People were mad.

And I felt fine.

Better than fine, really.

The world was my oyster and I hadn't a single care in the world.

Really, the happiness bubbling inside me only intensified as more and more realizations hit me throughout the day. Suicide hadn't even knocked on the door, and my ears were clean of any unseen speakers. Dipping further into the day and I realized that I hadn't hallucinated the first unwelcome guest. Not even Lady Death, my one welcome friend sprung from my imagination, graced me with her presence.

I'd certainly miss her. Lady Death was my one support who knew the extent of my madness. Maron was my best friend, but even she was unaware of how far gone I had been. Only the death's head hawk moth knew, and now she was gone.

I hoped she was okay.

Perhaps she found another damned soul to save.

Or maybe she ceased to exist.

Either way, it had been for the best.

After all, I think my winged friend's aim was for me to seize the bravery needed to traverse through the mucky waters of reality. She succeeded, too. I left class with my head held high and with an extra pep in my step. I hadn't the patience for angry fools, for I aimed for a move that the old Melbourne Thompson would've never made.

Through the peers leaving the very classroom I had emerged from, I approached one such soul who I figured would be a kindred spirit. He had to have been, of course. He, too, had received medical blessings from TerraCure. Tom Baxter couldn't have expected to keep his secrets forever.

"Tom!" I called out as I spotted him readying his hand to pull onto the door to the men's restroom. He looked up in my direction with partially widened eyes. I jogged up to him, in which he began to visibly clam up. "Hey, Tom," I greeted, stopping in front of him. "Long time, no see."

Tom grinned sheepishly. "Um. Yeah. I..." he rubbed the back of his head with his free hand. "Come here for a moment," he uttered quietly as he crept into the bathroom. I followed him, stepping swiftly into the room before the door could even close.

Sadly, we weren't alone in what was considered one of the most private places on campus. Well, any bathroom would fit that bill, I suppose. But the point still stood. The only people who would know our business would've been guys bored enough to listen in quietly.

Tom clearly understood the notion well, as evidenced by the conversational approach he took with me. "How about that new burger place downtown, Melbourne? I saw you there a few days ago."

I tilted my head in confusion at first, but quickly caught on once he winked at me. "Yeah dude," I said happily. "That place has some of the best fucking burgers I've ever eaten."

He smirked. "Yeah, I thought so, too. I got a cheeseburger with extra pickles."

I waggled my eyebrows, hoping the pickles were some kind of innuendo. "I got a cheeseburger, no mustard mixed into the ketchup."

Tom chuckled nervously as the last two dudes left the bathroom. A wave of relief washed over us both once we noticed that all of the well-tuned eardrums were gone. He breathed deeply and I smiled.

"Glad to hear TerraCure was good for you," he murmured. "I was just let out two days ago. I saw you there getting your dose."

I gave him a toothy grin, shedding all regret that might've stemmed from my next words. "Did you like what you saw?"

Tom squinted at me. "You mean in the tank, or..." Once he realized that my smile wasn't shrinking, his eyes widened and he looked down at the floor. "Err, I, uh. I mean, of course you didn't mean it like *that*."

"Didn't I?" I asked coyly, flashing him a wink. "I certainly liked what I saw when *you* were in that tank."

He instantly started coughing whilst chuckling weakly. The sight before me encouraged me greatly. The guy was flustered. He clearly didn't expect me to come on to him that strongly. Old Melbourne wouldn't have had the guts to put themself out there.

"Um, I, uh," Tom stammered, awkwardly rubbing the back of his head. "I-I think you have the wrong idea about me, Melbourne."

"Oh?" I asked with a subtle purr. "Am I mistaken, Tom? Or are you just bashful?"

He breathed deeply. "I'm not gay, dude."

I waggled my eyebrows again, making it clear that I wasn't going to give up that easily. If he legitimately felt uncomfortable around me, I would've instantly backed off. I wasn't one to prey on defenseless men or women.

But Tom wanted me.

I knew he did.

I always had an inkling.

But with TerraCure, I had the courage to call him out.

"I'm not a man, Tom. Nor am I a woman."

Tom chuckled nervously before clearing his throat. "I don't understand how that works, Melbourne. How can you be neither a man nor a woman?"

I took a step toward my love interest, lowering my voice in an amorous display of affection. "I'm what's called *a human.* Downstairs doesn't matter when passion is involved."

As I inched closer to his face, I noticed the bright pink blushing dabbed into his cheeks. My charm had an impact on him and that fact alone seemed to excite me in more ways than one. Old me had the charm of a drunken hobo begging for spare change. Who was this new Melbourne? I didn't recognize them and, honestly, I enjoyed their company.

"Melbourne," he said with a raspy croak. "We can't."

Not wasting another moment, I gently tugged onto the collar of his shirt and pulled him in for a kiss. My eyes closed and I allowed hot breaths to transfer from my mouth to his. He didn't hold me at first, as I'm sure he was caught off-guard. I might've had a similar reaction, had the tables been turned.

But Tom soon caved in.

He cupped my face and pulled me even closer to him; so close that our teeth barely grazed each other. I hummed happily. I'd done it. I'd snagged myself a lover worthy of my affection.

Once the kiss had been broken, Tom looked at me with hungry eyes. "Get in that stall," he ordered me. "*Now.*"

I shivered with anticipation. "I love when you order me around."

With that comment, Tom shoved me into an open stall. Once he followed, he locked the door behind him. I looked at him with depraved eyes, matching his own eager gaze. What a sexy, sexy man this Tom Baxter was.

And so the kissing continued, followed by desperate touching.

Clothes eventually came off, and we rutted in that bathroom.

Deep breaths.

Sensual gasps.

Fiery passion with each move.

The only being I cared for more than Tom was this new Melbourne Thompson. This person was a smooth criminal. They knew how to use their words to get what they wanted. A lover was the first step. Who knew what was next?

| twenty two |

A Crisp Mind

I was in Dr. Barris's class bright and early the next day. So early, in fact, that the sun was still rising as I stood outside the classroom. I stood alone in that hallway for quite some time, enjoying the refreshing silence inside my mind. I found solace in the loneliness, and I knew a few easy breaths would've been enough to sate the pounding snare drum within my ribcage.

I leaned against the eggshell wall, tapping my foot to a song playing in my head. I hadn't been one for old dad rock, but I still found myself tapping to the beat of *Do it Again* by Steely Dan. It reminded me of my parents, who were, no doubt, still angry with me. Back in the old days, I'd sit shotgun in my dad's roofless Jeep while he blasted old rock songs from the seventies and eighties.

Gone were the days of singing along with Steppenwolf.

Gone were the days of making guitar noises to mimic the solo in *Freebird.*

I was all grown up and on my dad's shitlist.

I would've been depressed if I hadn't been dancing in the honeymoon suite shared by TerraCure and myself.

As I tapped my foot, I looked all around me, wondering if I could see anything that hadn't been there before. My second full day of TerraCure had been proving to be filled with more blessings. Still not the first hallucination since I had stepped out of that tank. True, I was still in the infancy of my new life. For all I knew, the hallucinations would return in a matter of hours.

But that was later, though.

I wanted to dwell on the present for just a little longer.

I began to whistle just as my phone buzzed in my left pants pocket. I reached within and illuminated the screen. The message was from Maron, who seemed to have not gotten over her fury from yesterday. *"Mel, where are you?"*

I casually texted back, *"Waiting for class to start. What's up?"*

As I sent the text, I closed my eyes with a serene hum. Silence and still air sounded so satisfying to me. I'd always been told that a quiet mind begets a peaceful soul and enlightened mind, as per Buddhist teachings. I wasn't one for religion or spiritual know-how, but I had always wanted to change that. Perhaps I could've, now that I had peace of mind.

Maron texted back within a few moments, to which I held the phone up to read. *"I'm worried about you. You can't just leave for a week with no word. People are going to ask. People are going to wonder and worry."*

I sighed. Of course she was worried. *"I was gone for four days when I was in the hospital,"* I argued. *"Nobody gave a fuck."*

Within a few minutes, Maron responded. "*That was four days, Mel. That's not the same thing as a week.*"

"*It might as well be,*" I responded, quickly losing my patience. "*My absence has no bearing on anyone else's lives, Maron. Don't pretend that it does.*"

As I sent the message, I closed my eyes and thought about what I had said. Did I sincerely believe that nobody cared about me while I was gone? Surely, old me would've felt that way. Old me *did* feel that way. But perhaps that feeling was starting to wane.

I was loved.

I knew that.

But I also paid no mind to the worries of others.

Not anymore, anyway.

The phone buzzed again, to which I held the phone up and read. "*What's gotten into you? Of course people care! Where were you, even? You still haven't told me!*"

I rolled my eyes. "*That literally doesn't matter. All that matters is that I'm alive.*"

I sent the message and shoved the phone back in my pocket. I understood why she was upset, though I heavily disagreed with her reasoning. If Maron was truly my friend, she would've supported my last-ditch effort to better myself. Wasn't self-improvement the most vital goal of them all?

Whatever, I thought to myself.

Maron could cry all she wanted.

My life was mine; nobody else's.

"Not gonna let it bother me," I muttered to myself. "I'm not. I'm really not."

Before long, Dr. Barris entered the building and headed toward the classroom. He didn't notice me, as he seemed more fixated on the ground beneath his feet. I watched him, curious as to what might've been traversing through that membrane of his. Taxes? His love life? The ridiculously high bill his mechanic served him for fixing his car? Old me would've kept my mouth shut, but new me?

"Morning, Dr. B."

The professor jumped, jolted from whatever fascinated him so much on the floor. He looked at me with wide eyes, like a cat watching a stick swing a line of thread. "*Oh!* Melbourne? W-What are you doing here so early?"

"Thought I'd make up for lost time," I said with a grin. "Granted, I don't think I'd be keen on staying after class. Neither would you, I don't think."

He gave me a blank stare before clearing his throat. "Your final grade will determine your options, Melbourne. Much of what you missed will be covered, come exam time. I recommend you study hard."

I cackled, throwing my arms out. "What do you take me for, Dr. B? A slacker? Even before I was out, I--"

"Ran out of my class," the professor says, monotone and stone-faced. "Babbled incorrect explanations in class. Oh, and no-showed a week's worth of class with only a rather cryptic doctor's note."

I cocked an eyebrow. "What do you mean by that?"

"I don't need to explain it, Melbourne," Dr. Barris said, shaking his head. "You gave it to me. You know what it said and what it looked like."

I crossed my arms. "I thought it was pretty straightforward. It said I was out for a week due to a medical procedure."

"Yes," he responded. "It did say that, and nothing else. Not even a proper letterhead from an actual doctor's office."

"It was a signed note," I argued. "Besides, you accepted the note, didn't you? You told me I didn't have to do my homework."

He signed, now crossing his arms. "Only because I looked up the name and it appeared to belong to a new medical group called Aeon Industries. The Dean approved their request to be treated as a doctor's office. I couldn't just go against that, lest I be sued or fired."

I winked at the cynical man. "Well, allow me to say you're stuck with me until the end of class. Might as well enjoy it while it lasts."

Dr. Barris snorted. "Do your homework, go to class, pay attention, and pass your exams. Then I'll go easy on you."

I grinned from ear to ear. Despite having my oxygen crammed with the negativity of others, I felt confident. I knew everyone was there to doubt me. My family, my friends, and my teachers thought good old Melbourne was a pushover and that I loved it; how wrong could one be before it circled back around to being right?

"Take your seat," Dr. Barris muttered as he entered the classroom. I followed and did as I was told. A couple more classmates joined after a few minutes. Within several minutes of waiting patiently for class to start, the professor loudly cleared his throat, which halted the conversation amongst my peers. "Good morning, everyone. I trust you've all read last night's chapter on developmental theory."

Silence amongst the class.

Either everyone had read it, or they were just realizing that they forgot to do so.

I smiled, as I only skimmed through the pages and was still certain I knew the material.

"Seeing as how you're all such diligent students," he continued. "We're going to do some review before moving on with the next topic," He propped himself up against his desk. "So, who can tell me what happens to a child when they fail to satisfy the present stage of development, per Freud's theory of psychosexual development?"

A girl on the other side of the room raised her hand. "They develop a fixation?"

"Excellent, Ashley," Dr. Barris praised. "What sort of behaviors do adults exhibit whenever they've developed an oral fixation during their childhood?"

"They pick up bad habits that involve using their mouth," Tom spoke up. "Such as nail biting or smoking."

I smiled at the handsome man.

I'd show him a real oral fixation later in the evening.

"Good job, Tom," the professor said with a nod. "What about an anal fixation?"

I looked around the room. Nobody raised their hand. I was surprised that this question, amongst a grocery list of complicated concepts, was what stumped the class. And so, to save the class from being berated from a cantankerous man, I raised my hand.

"People with anal fixations usually are a lot grouchier and obsessive about certain things, such as cooking and cleaning," I grinned evilly. "They also tend to be very cranky for no real reason. They may even get a job as a college professor."

My comment gave a few classmates a chuckle as Dr. Barris aggressively cleared his throat. "*Yes*, Melbourne. Thank you for that," he lifted himself from his desk. "Can anyone give me a general synopsis on what nature versus nurture entails?"

My hand shot up again. "Children can develop certain problems or habits when surrounded by those influences for too long. Kind of like if a child is beaten everyday. They may grow up to be afraid of parental figures. Certain problems may be caused by nature, or genetics, too. But nurture seems to do much of the heavy lifting."

Dr. Barris nodded. "Good. I see you've been studying."

"Of course," I commented. "I'm especially hyped for today's lesson. I read ahead in the textbook. Hope you don't mind."

The professor crossed his arms. "Really? In that case, give us a brief synopsis on what the chapter is about."

I stood up from my chair and cleared my throat. "The lesson covers theory of mind. It's essentially what helps us understand how each of us is different. We all have our opinions, interests, thoughts, feelings, and so forth. Children who develop theory of mind learn empathy. They realize that those around them are just as important as they, themselves, are."

The professor nodded. "That's a fairly good--"

"It's been said that those with psychosis struggle with theory of mind," I continued. "But I think that's a flawed stance to have. Psychotic people are more than capable of experiencing empathy. Theory of mind is clearly a concept that psychologists need to spend more time researching, as it seems a little behind the times."

A couple of my peers looked back at me. Tom smirked and winked at me. Dr. Barris cleared his throat again, albeit slower than before. "Very good, Melbourne. Perhaps I should let *you* teach the class today."

I chuckled. "No thank you, sir. But I think I have a topic for my research paper now."

He forced a grin. "So you do, Melbourne. So you do."

Pride swelled up within me like a balloon. As the insanity had been flushed from my system, I was now sharper, smarter. At the rate I was going, I was more than likely going to graduate valedictorian in a few years. I'd surely be the top of my class.

I could hardly wait.

| twenty three |

Ambition, Shattered

If my intellectual prowess was something to behold, I only briefly imagined how much more would change in the athletic sense. My body looked the same as it had before the procedure, but were things still wired the same way? Was I destined to get jacked within two arm and leg days at the gym? Would I be the fastest human being to have ever walked the planet?

All of these possibilities sprung up inside my head as I rolled my pant legs up to my knees. I had no desire to go into the locker room. While it would've been a treat to see all of the muscular men baring their fruit to the entire world, TerraCure had turned me into a sex machine. The things Tom and I had done in that precious moment together would go with me until the end of time. My virginity was never to return and I knew I wouldn't miss it.

Alas, I had class to attend to.

There wasn't any time for loving.

As I pulled my white socks up, I stood up straight and examined my surroundings. Today was rugby, which the boys were conflicted about. "Why not football?" some would ask. "It's football for *real* men!" others would crow. I didn't even know how to play rugby, so I was at a disadvantage either way.

A whistle was blown suddenly, bringing my attention to the middle of the gym floor. "Line up," commanded the physical education teacher, Mrs. Burns.

I jogged up to the horizontal line forming a couple feet from the elderly, yet unnecessarily strong woman. She was no doubt the first and only gray-hair I've seen that was completely jacked. By no means was she a bodybuilder, but she could absolutely kick my and probably every able-bodied athlete in the school's ass if need be. I wondered if TerraCure had made me strong enough to take her in a brawl.

"C'mon everyone," she called out, clapping her hands. "I could've scarfed down an entire burger by now. Let's *go!*"

About twelve of us, four girls, six guys, and I, stood side-by-side as we observed the old woman digging into her left pants pocket. She pulled out a ring of keys and jingled them in front of us. "See these? These are the keys to the gym closet," Mrs. Burns tossed them up and down into her palm. "I want you guys to decide what we do today. I'm throwing the ball into your court."

Two guys chuckled at the pun and the girls rolled their eyes. I watched the keys as the woman's wrist bounced the ring up and down. "I thought we were doing rugby today," I commented aloud. A few of the boys agreed with my sentiment, talking amongst themselves.

"Correct," Mrs. Burns said. "I did initially plan for you guys to play rugby. However, things change," she glared at what I assumed was a fly off in the distance. "Especially when drunk frat boys steal the ball needed to play rugby and toss it into the murky lake by the library."

My eyebrows rose, though mostly out of faux shock. Campus antics didn't surprise me too much, though I was admittedly taken aback by the elderly woman's brazen observation that may or may not have been completely true. I knew all about beliefs that were only partially based in reality. I half wondered if Mrs. Burns suffered from delusions. It wouldn't have been too out of line to assume the old woman was losing her marbles, right?

"Now," the gym instructor said. "Before we choose a game, I want you lightweights to drop and give me twenty. Whoever finishes first will be the lucky soul who picks a game from the ball closet."

A few of the guys started groaning. "This is stupid," one muttered.

"It's either that," the elderly woman said, not missing a beat. "Or you boys help tend the campus garden while us ladies sip on frozen lemonade while watching you."

The girls each started giggling. "Picking flowers might be too hard for them, Mrs. Burns," commented one; a girl with a red ponytail. "Wouldn't want them to prick themselves on thorns or anything. Everybody knows how delicate guys are."

Half of the men awkwardly looked down at their feet while the other half glared at the red-head who had dared challenge their machismo. Me? I found myself chuckling. Joke was on them; I didn't mind gardening. I helped my mother pull weeds occasionally as well as water her azaleas.

Gone were those days, I thought to myself.

Maybe my folks would find it in their hearts to forgive me.

Key detail being *one day.*

"We'll show you fucking *delicate*," growled a muscular, tan dude. "Drop and give you twenty? How about drop and give you thirty?"

A mischievous grin swept across the old woman's face. "Why stop at thirty, Sam? Whoever can give me the most push-ups can choose our game," she glanced over at the girls. "That goes for you too, ladies. Don't let a bunch of men outshine you."

I remained quiet during the competitive shit talk. I wasn't a woman, but I wasn't a man, either. I was a team of one, me versus the binary. Did I think I could take them all on? Absolutely!

"Everyone drop to the floor on the count of three," Mrs. Burns instructed, holding the metal whistle up to her face. "One, two..." She blew into her whistle, creating a loud squeal to slam hard into the walls around us. With the final echoes, we all dropped to the floor.

Before TerraCure, my attempts to drop to my hands and tip-toes were always in vain. I'd try to catch myself, but ultimately end up face-planting into the gym floor. Giving *one* was too difficult, let alone twenty, ten, or even five. The only thing that would hurt more than my body was my pride.

But I had risen above those dark days. When I dropped onto the floor that day, I effortlessly caught myself and began to push myself just centimeters from the floor. I then pushed myself upward, and back down. I repeated this movement over and over again, gradually speeding up over the seconds.

My body didn't ache.

Struggle was an urban legend.

To my left were the girls, and to my right were the boys. In my peripheral vision, I noticed that three out of four girls had given up after five to ten push-ups. The fourth girl, who just so happened to be the sassy red-head, soldiered on to complete her twenty before dropping onto the floor for good.

Meanwhile, four of the guys had succumbed to rest after ten to fifteen push-ups. Telltale whimpers emulated in my ears as their pride eviscerated right before my eyes. One guy grunted loudly as he managed to break twenty and carry on to at least twenty-five.

It was then down to the tan dude and myself. We both had broken twenty push-ups and were well on our way to breaking thirty. As we committed to the workout, I glanced over at him. He looked back at me with a cocky smile. "Give up, faggot. I got this in the bag."

I laughed loudly as I winked at him, not even thinking about the workout anymore. It was as if my body was on autopilot. "We'll see about that, you jockey motherfucker."

Once we broke forty, I could hear his struggle starting to materialize. He huffed hoarsely, swearing under his breath. Once we broke forty-five, his agony grew much louder. "*Shit*! Fuck me!"

At fifty push-ups, I decided to show off by placing one hand behind my back. Even with only one arm holding me up, I still felt no pain or exhaustion. The muscular man looked at me with his mouth agape. "How are you doing that?!"

I chuckled as I witnessed him finally drop to the ground once and for all. "That's for me to know and for you to question," I broke fifty-five and gave him another wink. "A question you'll never receive an answer to."

With everyone down, I found myself on the fence over a simple action. Should I have stopped? I had won. I didn't need to show off anymore. Nobody was going to question my strength at that point, right?

I guess I doubted myself even then. Instead of succumbing to the cold floor, I continued to push myself up and down. Once I broke sixty, I could hear the surprised gasps around me. "Very impressive, Melbourne," Mrs. Burns exclaimed happily. "I never knew you had it in you."

With a cocky grin of my own, I didn't stop there. I ventured forth and found myself breaking sixty-five, then seventy, and then seventy-five. I felt completely fine. No pain in my muscles or bones. No sweat dropping into malodorous puddles beneath me. I was a machine, well-oiled with tightly bolted gears. This engine was never going to give in to the illusion of rest.

"Okay, that's enough," Mrs. Burns commented. I ignored her and went on to break eighty push-ups. "Melbourne, we get it. You're strong. You can stop now." I, again, ignored her pleas. I soon broke eighty-five and then ninety. My goal was to stop right at one-hundred. After all, I only had ten push-ups to go. Why wouldn't I aim big?

It wasn't until I broke ninety-five that my body finally started to ache. I thought it was nothing to be concerned about initially. Alas, the pain grew rapidly with each push-up.

Ninety-six, my arms began to wobble.

Ninety-seven, sharp needles began to stab at my muscles.

Ninety-eight, I began to gasp for air.

Ninety-nine, I heard the others heckle me.

They told me I couldn't make it to one-hundred, but I proved them wrong. I knew I could do it. However, my body reacted in a way that never in my wildest dreams would I have expected it to. At one-hundred, I began to scream.

The flesh around my forearms began to rip and tear, revealing pulsating tissue. My biceps suddenly grew three times their original size. And then, much to my horror, another set of arms began to sprout from my sides. Those arms grew hands, which planted themselves onto the floor and held me up through the ungodly pain.

I had hoped it was just another hallucination, a freak thing that TerraCure couldn't quite fix. But my hopes were for naught. Everyone around me began to scream; even the boys.

"Holy shit!"

"Oh my God!"

"What the fuck?!"

Everyone, including Mrs. Burns, sprinted out of the gymnasium. I didn't know what was going on. Why was this happening? *What* was happening?

Lest I became a sideshow freak of nature, I pulled myself up with all four of my arms and quickly rushed to Phil and Ian's lab.

| twenty four |

Nails in the Coffin

All eyes on me, the freak of nature known as Melbourne Thompson. My four arms crossed over my torso and waist, trying hopelessly to blend in with my clothes. I needed some solitude. I needed something to keep the eyes off me, anything to keep the screams down to a minimum.

But nothing was so simple. No matter how hard I tried to cover myself up and keep my extra appendages concealed, at least one person would see through the camouflage. Their scream would trigger more screams which, in turn, would trigger a horde or two of frightened students running for the hills. That horde would separate into a second horde, and then that horde separated into a third and forth horde.

I was Frankenstein's monster, in the flesh.

And my body wasn't even done.

No, the gruesome transformation continued even as I ran.

The hair on my original set of arms started to grow out, coating my flesh with dark fur. Soon, my second pair of arms began to do the same. I'm certain my legs followed suit, if the prickly sensation run-

ning down my pant legs was any indicator. I half-expected to grow fangs and take on a more bestial visage. If I was going to change into something scary, why not a werewolf?

Unfortunately, no such luck walked toward me.

I screamed again as a hump in my back started to rise up like a hilltop. Right as I had made it to the door to the science building, I dropped as my posture forcibly curved downward so I was hunched over. My shirt ripped completely off me as my panicked hands grabbed onto the door handle. I opened it mid-scream as another surge of pain coursed through me, this time in my lower back, just above my haunches.

Much to my short-lived relief, I was the only being within the lobby. As my pants and underwear had both been blown off of me during the materialization of what appeared to be a tail, my second set of arms censored my exposed genitalia from the cruel world. I fought through the agony and approached the door to Aeon Industries, my footsteps loud and heavy.

I groaned loudly as I opened the door. I screamed and cried so hard that my voice no longer sounded like my own. It sounded like something akin to a monster in a horror movie. I was unable to even close the door behind before I dropped to my knees once again, wailing like a banshee.

A pretty blonde girl sat in a chair within the entrance, playing on her phone. She didn't appear to be doing any sort of preparation for a procedure. My assumption was that this girl was Rachel. Either way, she very much noticed my entrance and dropped her cellular device onto the floor.

"Oh my god!" she screamed before leaping out of her seat. "Ian? Phil?!"

I slowly clamored back to my feet. "*Fix me,*" I commanded, voice straining against the constant pain. "Please...*help me.*"

The girl shrieked just before running to the back of the lab. "Guys?! Guys, please! We have a situation!"

The muscles in my thighs pulsated as my calves begin to grow some meat. I moaned in pain as I shuffled down past the orange tubes. Before I could make it to the end, I felt something hot poke me in the small of my back, just above my tail. The heat didn't phase me, but the electrical shocks surging through my nervous system successfully dropped me onto the floor.

"Grab his legs," came the voice of Phil. "C'mon, Rachel. *Grab his fucking legs!*"

Another shock stunned me as Ian showed up from behind the blonde. He wielded what appeared to be a stocky, black gun. Shooting from its barrel was a line of sparks. The bastard had fired a fucking taser at me.

"Help..." I pleaded as Rachel held onto my thick legs. "Help...me. *Help me!*"

As Ian kept his taser aimed at me, I noticed that Phil looked down at me. His expression didn't communicate shock or even horror. If anything, he seemed intrigued...dare I say amused?

"Hello, Melbourne Thompson," he greeted calmly. "I see TerraCure has begun to shape you into the kind of man you aspire to be."

I squinted at the attractive scientist. "N-No...I d-don't want this!"

"But you do, though," Phil argued. "You wanted to fix your brain. You wanted to be less of a madman," the blonde man smiled down upon me. "You'll find that your mind has never been sharper."

I roared angrily. "That doesn't...mean...mean...I..."

"You thought your mind was your only imperfection, I'm guessing?" Ian asked, still aiming the taser at me. "You wanted a clean mind, but didn't think to look in the mirror and understand that you were in need of a clean body, as well."

I forced my eyes shut as another wave of pain flushed over me. "Y-You! You said!"

Phil chuckled. "I *did* say, yes. But what you have to realize, Melbourne...do you prefer being called Melbourne? Or Mel? Mr. Thompson?"

I wailed loudly.

"*Ahhh,*" Phil mimicked. "Okay, now I know what to call you."

"Phil," Rachel said quietly. "What is this? Is this a glitch, or..."

"Call it a step," Ian answered. "The fourth step, more specifically."

I blinked slowly.

Fourth?

What were the first, second, and third steps?

"You see," the poindexter continued. "Perfection is completely achievable, and TerraCure is precisely what is needed to attain it."

"But what *is* perfection?" Phil asks. "Is it the clean brain, silky smooth skin, or immaculate figure?" The blonde scientist shook his head. "To be strong is to look strong. To be sane is to look sane. You have the latter down pat, but you still looked like a shrimp. TerraCure aims to fix every little imperfection you have. This college campus was our testing ground. Pretty soon, the rest of the town will receive TerraCure. Before you know it, the state, then country, and then world may also be privileged enough to have our serum."

I clenched my teeth, whole body shaking. "You...you think *this* is perfect?!"

Phil held his hand up and lifted his index finger. "Step one: realizing that you are imperfect," he lifted his middle finger next. "Step two: ingest TerraCure. Ingest as much as you can."

"Step three," Ian continued. "Reap the rewards of the mind," he smirked as he finally lowered his weapon. "Step four: reap the rewards of the body."

"You call this perfect?!" I screamed frantically. "I'm a freak! An abomination! Please! Please fix me!"

"You don't really want to be..." Phil said, lifting his hands up and bending his fingers to resemble quotations. "Fixed. After all, you'd end up back to your old, psychotic self. Your hallucinations would come back, and you'd continue to be alone and misunderstood. Do you really want that?"

I hyperventilated. My options were to be crazy or forever look like a monster. If I had known that this was my future when committing to the TerraCure serum, I would've never spent so much time obsessing over it. I would've just committed suicide like I had originally planned.

"Besides," Phil said with a wicked grin. "If *you're* transforming now, it must mean all of the other patients are, too."

Right on cue, the loud shrieks of students outside the room lingered like elevator music. Really, I believed the screaming was coming from outside the building, possibly all around the campus.

An uprising was happening.

Aeon Industries planned it perfectly.

They wielded paintbrushes and worked to paint the entire campus an entirely new color.

That color, and all of its shades, resembled their delusional idea of perfection.

twenty five

Ground Zero

I moved as fast as my transfigured form could manage in my attempts to break away from the psychopathic scientists. Rachel didn't even attempt to put up a fight when I jerked around. She let go of me and quickly backed away. "Should I blast him again, Phil?" Ian asked, aiming the taser at my head as I forced myself onto my pulsating, disgustingly enlarged feet.

"No," the handsome blonde said calmly. "I want to see where this goes. Let our hard work pay off."

As I stood up, my hunched back ached as the pain continued to beat the tissue within my flesh like it were a drum set used by the world's angriest drummer. I frantically turned around and rushed out of the laboratory, dreading the monstrous sight that was sure to greet me from outside the science building's walls. As the pain intensified, I found myself struggling to even stand straight. The pads of my feet stung with each step I took. It wouldn't be long until I could no longer run.

I crashed through the entrance doors, my body mass tearing them off the hinges. I squawked loudly as I looked at the campus around me. The smell of smoke caressed my nostrils, making me turn to my left. The smell was no hallucination, a fact that I found myself lamenting.

Many of the office buildings burned around me and crowds of students ran in every direction in the attempt to seek shelter. Everyone who ran toward me immediately freaked out and turned away; some even tripped over each other. "No..." I groaned loudly as the back of my eyes began to sting. "What did--"

The flesh around my neck ripped.

Blood gushed all over me.

I screamed as my neck shot up several feet.

My head was well above me when my eyes literally popped out of their sockets.

"For f-fuck's sake," I shrieked, unable to blink away the sun's angry stare. "What have they done?!"

With one hard step, my ankles gave out on me. With another yelp, I fell onto my knees. The nerve of Aeon Industries, bragging about their sick idea of perfection. If they wanted me to be powerful, why did it hurt to run? Why was walking such a chore? Even when I was standing, pins and needles crunched down on my feet.

"Oh my fucking God," shouted a guy who was accompanied by three cheerleaders. Judging by his attire, he seemed to be affiliated with the football team. His physique, however, made it perfectly clear that he wasn't one of the players. Maybe he was a waterboy? I supposed it didn't matter, anyway.

"Pl-Please," I begged as he and the girls stared at me in justifiable terror. "Don't run. Please listen to me!"

A cheerleader with dyed purple hair whipped out some pepper spray from her cleavage and aimed it at me. Her movements were so fast that I could understand completely how she got on the team. "S-Stay back," she breathed fearfully. "D-Don't make me use this!"

I glanced down at the pink spray, its white nozzle staring me down like we were in a Mexican stand-off. My burning eyes dared not to challenge the young woman. Her friends hid behind her, even the waterboy. I felt like an alien with my dangling eyes, my long neck, and overly muscular body.

My observation suggested fear.

Fear begets anger.

Anger begets hunger.

Ravenous hunger for her hair and flesh.

I couldn't even bring myself to feel nausea over my definite disgust and shame. Was I even capable of throwing up anymore, or was my body too perfect to succumb to illness? How could I so casually acknowledge newfound cannibal instincts without screaming once more?

Because I wasn't a human anymore.

Eating those students would've been like eating chicken for most people.

I bared my teeth and jumped on top of the cheerleader. "Help me," she screamed as she dropped her pepper spray and began slapping me with both of her hands. Her fellow cheerleaders rushed to my sides and attempted to pry my massive body off her. The waterboy backed away slowly, horror tattooed onto his face.

I shoved the two girls away from me, pushing them hard enough to knock them onto the ground. I wasted no time in biting down on her face. She let out the most blood curdling scream I'd ever heard in my entire life. Had I maintained even a shred of dignity, I would've let her go. She might've not had to succumb to such a grisly fate.

But her chances of survival were nonexistent.

As her skin peeled away, I clawed into her stomach, ripping it open. As her intestines spilled out, I pulled away from her and immediately noticed the waterboy running for his life. The other cheerleaders screamed loudly while they followed him. Just like that, the girl was abandoned; left to die alone at the hands of a beast.

This was the new me. My mind might've been free of psychosis, but my bodily autonomy certainly wasn't. Ian and Phil said this was okay. They said it was perfect. Who was I to judge them? Why not give in to the new me?

My body chilled as warm blood coated the skin around my lips. I looked back down at the dead cheerleader. Her pretty face was now replaced with ugly tissue and exposed eyeballs. I smiled wide.

Maybe those scientists were right.

My mind was the alpha.

My body was the beta.

My soul was the omega.

All in one, I was the most perfect specimen on the face of the Earth.

| twenty six |

Her Favorite Flower

It was three days after the outbreak. Many students had fallen to their new overlords. The campus alone reeked of death, massacred bodies resting eternally on the ground. Some stragglers occasionally came out of hiding, likely to find food or a way to escape. Those people eventually fell, too.

There were around thirty of us, each with different gifts based on their own personalized administered TerraCure treatment. The weak-bodied were blessed with big muscles and unmatched stamina. The strong-bodied's brains grew several sizes larger, allowing them to easily comprehend logistics and the likely psychological hurdles experienced by our prey. This included any possible escape plans they might've conjured up after hours of deliberation.

No holes in the ground fooled us.

Nor silent footsteps.

Nor smooth-talking.

We were their betters in every way.

The hunters always won.

To make matters worse for the hunted, my people and I had our own language. Was it foreign? No; it just utilized vocabulary that the average human could not understand. Some might've been intelligent enough to know what we were saying, sure. Of course, that flex didn't last long due to my people's usage of code words.

Think substitution, but with categorical switches. Instead of asking for directions, we were instructing others on how to pave roads. In the case of my campus, we often misled survivors by saying we were doing one thing when we were actually setting up traps. Tom was good at this, especially. He sent eavesdropping students to the library by stating his squad was going to patrol the classrooms across the campus.

Both were learning areas.

Knowledge found in classrooms was given by others.

Knowledge found in the library was earned.

Which was better, I wondered.

Patrolling the school grounds was best done in a pack, though flying solo wasn't so terrible, either. Johnny and Kimberly, of course, often opted to stick close to one another. Even in this new life, they were meant to be. I hoped Tom and I could make it to that point one day. One step at a time.

On the third day, I traversed the grounds alone. It was my turn to comb through each of the buildings in search of survivors. We'd cleaned out most of them, but there was always more. We had no leader, so it wasn't like we were expected to meet some kind of quota. Honestly, I was simply itching to get first dibs on a fresh feast.

My first stop was the cafeteria, then the first swath of classrooms and closets. The bathrooms were empty, just like them. My vision was immaculate, so I knew I wasn't missing anything right in front of me; my enhanced hearing didn't defy me, either.

I soon found myself in Dr. Barris's old classroom. I hadn't seen him since the outbreak had occurred. Perhaps he quit his job and was now safe at home? Or maybe somebody managed to catch him and devour his entrails.

Lucky them, I thought to myself.

I wanted the satisfaction of eating that bastard.

Only a few of the tables had been flipped over during the initial attack. No blood smears or rotting carcasses. It almost looked normal. My old seat was intact, too.

Upon exiting the room, I heard a noise. The noise was something I hadn't heard in a very long time, even before I'd ever heard of TerraCure. It boomed off in the distance, my hearing pinning it around the old science building. I heard it once, and then heard it several more times in rapid succession.

Gunshots, likely from a nine-millimeter.

I smiled wickedly.

"Time for breakfast," I murmured as I bolted toward the source of the noise. My large leg muscles supported my even larger body, allowing me to run as fast as a gazelle. We all were like this, my pack and I. There was no wonder why so many had fallen at our feet.

Once I reached the science building, I crashed through the doors, just like I had three days ago. I was no longer panicked, however. I'd learned to love the bomb dropped onto my head. When I reached the open doorway leading into Aeon Industries, I realized that I was too late in thanking my creators.

Four bodies occupied the room, three of which were dead. Ian was sprawled out onto the floor beside the tubes, chest bleeding. Phil's predicament was no better, as he was hunched over a table, bloody bullet holes tattooed onto his white lab coat. The vials and beakers that had once occupied the surface were shattered onto the floor. Rachel's body laid near Phil's, a bloody pool forming underneath her.

It didn't take long for me to figure out who had killed them. The smell of a smokey barrel tickled my nose hairs, leading me to face an individual sitting on the floor, leaned up against an empty tube. A blonde girl with tattered jeans and a blue blouse, ripped at the collar to reveal the purple bra underneath. My eyes widened when I recognized her.

"Maron?"

My best friend viciously shook, tears pouring down her face as she hyperventilated. "S-Stay back," she pleaded, not even looking at my face. "I-I know h-how to use this."

"Maron, it's me," I said with a deepened voice. "Melbourne. Melbourne Thompson. We're besties, remember?"

With a visible loss of breath, she looked up at me slowly. She sobbed loudly once she met my eyes. "Mel...what have you done?"

I blinked at her. "What do you mean?"

"You know very fucking well what I mean," she shouted as her shaky hands pointed her gun at me. "Look at yourself, Mel! Look at everything--everyone around you! They're either dead or worse! How can you sleep at night?!"

I continued to stare at her. "Your smell is tantalizing."

Her eyes somehow managed to widen more than they had been. "Y-Your buddies are dead," she raised her voice, now screaming. "They're *gone*, Mel! They're gone!"

I bared my teeth. "They'll taste just like you, regardless."

She swallowed hard. "Please, Mel. Please! *Stop this*!"

With that, I roared loudly as I grabbed her. Her screams echoed in my ears as I bit into her neck. Ripping the flesh off her like a turkey dinner, I wasted no time in munching down on her body. Oddly enough, Maron's blood hit differently than other meals had. As I drank her, I noticed a sweeter taste. She still tasted like aluminum, but there was something else that just made her flavor so much better than the rest.

Maybe it was our bond that sweetened her?

Maybe she had a medical condition that altered the taste of her blood?

All I knew was that I'd never taste something so delectable ever again.

Once I had satisfied my hunger, I dropped what remained of Maron onto the floor. I took a moment to look down at her. Should I have said goodbye? Could the dead even speak? If they could, would she even acknowledge me? I suppose it didn't matter anymore. Not even an apology would suffice at that point.

Without saying a single word, I turned around and left the laboratory, soon trekking out into the wasteland known as the campus grounds. The morning sky darkened during my micro-adventure. Clouds loomed over my head. I always enjoyed the weather before storms. It wasn't cold, but not hot either. Goldilocks certainly had great taste, I realized.

Suddenly, another sound caught my attention. This one was much closer, much less violent. I looked to my right and noticed something small flying my way. It took me a moment to realize what I was looking at. It wasn't until I heard squeaking that I smiled wide.

Lady Death fluttered toward me, the flapping of her beautiful wings keeping her afloat. "Long time, no see," I greeted. "I guess you were real this whole time, huh?"

The moth looked at me, her expression foreign to me. Was she happy? Upset? Maybe pensive? All I could gather was that she was staring holes through me.

"Things have gone a little crazy since we last spoke, my friend," I chuckled weakly. "I'm sure you've noticed by now."

The squeak of the death's head hawk moth erupted like a volcano. It was loud enough to catch me off guard. I stumbled back. "Easy, girl. It's me. It's just me, Melbourne."

Lady Death continued to squeak a few more times as she whizzed around my head. I couldn't tell if she missed me, or if she was berating me like an angry mother. I suppose it could've been both. Last time she saw me, I was a scrawny human with a diseased mind. Now I was a hulking beast with a mind at ease.

"Are you trying to tell me something?" I asked. "You always have something helpful to say. What is it?"

Within a few more trips around my head, the moth flew away from me. "Wait," I called out to her before making the decision to follow behind. I dared not run, as I feared my velocity would squish her like a speeding truck. The speed of my walking even increased in my new form. It reminded me of my normal running speed during my past life.

I followed the moth closely, never taking my eyes off her. I needed to know what she was thinking. I didn't think I'd be able to sleep if I'd just chosen to ignore her. She and Maron both meant much to me before, but Maron was a human like everyone else. Lady Death, on the other hand, was my guardian angel.

She eventually stopped moving forward, floating in place. I waited to see what she'd do next. Like a supermodel, I found myself entranced by the majesty she emulated. She turned around to face me once more. It felt like we were the only living creatures left on Earth.

But within two blinks, she was gone.

The moth had disappeared right before my eyes.

"Death, wait!"

My cries went unheard, as my guardian angel seemingly evaporated into the wind like dust. Normally, she'd fly off and meet me somewhere later on. The moth didn't even fly that time, which told me that I'd never see her again.

Forlorn, I looked down at the ground. A small grin crept over my grotesque face as I realized that she had, in fact, left me a message. I hadn't realized it before, but she had taken me to a garden. More specifically, it was the garden that dressed the library. Only one kind of flower was planted in that particular garden: red spider lilies.

"What are *you* doing here?" I asked. "Your home is in Asia. Why are you so far from home?"

The flowers did not speak to me, not like Lady Death had many times before. Did she turn into these flowers, or did she simply lead me to them? Whatever was happening, a conflicted sensation rumbled within my ribcage, stinging my heart.

In my head, I saw gray; no other color but gray. Strange lights occasionally flashed, but nothing stayed. Black speckles floated around only for a few seconds after each flash. I hadn't the slightest idea what to make of it.

After a few minutes, a woman emerged from within the gray. She had long black hair and a long white gown. She didn't appear to be wearing any kind of shoes or make-up, but that was okay. She didn't need anything to make her beautiful; her natural beauty was already miles above the standard beauty queen.

She beckoned me to follow her, but I couldn't. My attempts to move my legs were in vain, as my feet felt like they'd been welded into the ground. I tried to speak to her, but my words were trapped in my throat. Only my eyes were able to communicate with her.

After a moment, she held her arms out. White sparkles emerged around her and she was suddenly cradling a baby. I wanted to ask her if that was her child, but my voice was, once again, rendered useless. The way she looked at that baby made my heart ache.

Why?

Why was I so sad?

Before I could make another attempt to ask, the woman turned away from me and started walking. I desperately tried to follow, but I couldn't. No matter what I did, I couldn't move my feet. Within seconds, the woman and child were gone.

Tears rolled down my eyes. Without them, I was alone. Despite the separation I'd had with Lady Death, I felt the silence cripple me. I wished I could hear her squeaks again. I wished I could learn more from her. If not Lady Death, then I could've heard Maron's laughter one more time.

But I needed to move forward. All I had now was my pack, my bloodlust. It was only a matter of time until we abandoned the school grounds in search of fresh food. There were many overpopulated cities that needed to be thinned. Perhaps we'd traverse across different states, or maybe even countries.

That would've been a long time from then. For that moment, all I had were my memories; bitter, bitter memories. Everyone I loved was gone. My friends were decimated and my family would surely meet a similar fate in due time.

All I had left was my pack.

The only beauty left were the red spider lilies.

Within time, however, they too would vanish before my eyes.

Nash Nelson is a self-published author. Always eager to exercise his freedom as a writer, he writes gritty, dark fiction for adults. Per his website:

"From the southern United States, I have always wanted to be a writer. Ever since I was a small child, I took every opportunity possible to write silly stories for my family to read; be it on our old Windows 2000 computer or stapled pieces of construction paper.

My education is in Psychology, but my passion has always been in literature. I was told from a young age that I could be anything I wanted…only for me to turn 18 and have my parents tell me that I needed to get a "real" college degree. Funny how that works!

While I've been writing for years, I published my first book in March of 2021. I hope to increase my portfolio of written works in the years to come! :)"